Life's Novellas

Fate

Waits

Upon

No

One

Books by the Anonymous Author and Artist

Their Poetic Minds

Poems are juxtaposed, religiously, femininely, and dichotomously.

Poems of Life

Poems are mixed schematically, stylistically, and randomly.

Life's Heart Break: *A Novella*

In the end, will Zenald discover what may be one of life's biggest heart-breaks: heart-ache?

Duty and Destruction I

A real female experiences life in and out of the U.S. military.

Life's Poetic Dichotomies

Some of life's biggest dichotomies are juxtaposed poetically.

Her Poetic Rise

It is for the religiously poetic that blends religion and feminism.

Life's Short Stories

Fictional characters vie to live their own lives.

Life's Mixed Poetry

Poems are mixed schematically, stylistically, and randomly.

Art Book

The Diamond & Heart Art Collections

Pictures are exhibited, categorically, by coloring schemes and coloring mediums; all of which, have been affected with special effects.

Schemes: pastel shades; earth tones; primary colors; gray, black and white; black and white.

Mediums: colored pencils; water coloring; pastel coloring; acrylic coloring; oil coloring.

Life's Novellas

Fate
Waits
Upon
No
One

Anonymous

Century Conquests

Life's Novellas

Fate Waits Upon No One

Copyright © 2012 by Anonymous

www.centuryconquests.com
info@centuryconquests.com

ISBN: 978-0-9850698-5-8

Cover graphic designed by: Century Conquests © 2011

Century Conquests ® 2012

Life's Novellas

*Fate
Waits
Upon
No
One*

Anonymous

Acknowledgements

For, the very small voice so deep in me—that, once again, wants me to carry on, fictionally.

I thank, as well, all persons that have so helped with the publication of this book.

I most certainly thank each and every reader of my book, for permitting me the privilege of diverting your attention, or interest; and, beguiling you; and, even, allowing me to put into words, my artistic, creative, and literary logic.

Author's Note

This is a work of fiction. In addition, and assuming no responsibility for any figurative or literal mix-up; best efforts have been put forth; to actualize the actuality of historical, cultural, social, and, religious, and even, political, and the like; references, inferences, interpretations, and so forth—or, forces, that are contained here in.

Additionally, the publisher and the author both have had no necessary need to denigrate any, ("so-called, or otherwise"), human figure; or, a company's product; or even, a company's service; and so on, except, in the case of actual necessity.

…When the one great scorer comes to write against YOUR name, he writes not that you won or lost, but HOW you played the game.

—Anon

AKA
Anonymous

Book I: The Good

Fate

Waits

Upon

No

One

Prelude

Act I

Scene 1

San Diego, California

On a some-what cloudy, or gray, and damp, and even early—or, an un-inviting, Thursday morning or day in late fall of 2001; at a stylishly sizable home, right, on the outskirts of San Diego, California; the telephone rings aloud inside of the dark master-bedroom-suite.

DINNG!
DINNNG! "What…?" I question, tossing and turning on my awfully comfortable and king-sized bed. DINNNG: "Hold on—DAMIT…!" I shriek, soundly, and being awoken, so rudely, from a restlessly good night's sleep. I snatch the telephone from my bed stand: "Hello!" I screech, sitting up, some.

"Morning, Derrick. And, I'm so sorry about telephoning you so damn early. But, there's just never a good time to deliver sad or bad news—"

"Oh no…! What's so happened…?" I ask, and am anxious, or eager, somewhat.

The white, and middle-aged, and even long-time co-worker of a boss; or, Deputy Security Officer John Downs, of Aegis Associates, speaks, so un-easily, if not apologetically: "Well—ahhh, listen, I'm sorry—but, there's just no easy way to say it—"

"I'm being let go. Oh no…!"

"Yes … well, and regrettably so. Of course, we've talked about such possibility—"

"I know that. Yet, I just didn't expect such so 'damn' soon. Or, to be un-employed this 'goddamn' soon—'down—or, let down—or even let go!'" OH, NO…! Anxiety is now setting in; "Well, thanks for calling me…, John. I suppose, too, that I could or should return to work, today, to just clear out my belongings?" I state, questioningly, and, anxiously. For, it's something super serious to be utterly un-easy or nakedly nervous about: job-less-ness—or, un-employ-ment.

John now replies ironically—and, almost, certainly, moronically. "Go ahead and take the rest of the week off. You can return next week…. Also, Derrick, I aim, absolutely, to help you with your transition and all. Likewise, please, give my regards—and, regrets, to your lovely wife—*Xina*."

"Will do and thanks—"

"I thank you…. And, good-bye, for now."

"Bye-bye...," I finally end the utterly un-satisfactory, and, for damn sure, utterly un-welcoming conversation; which, I've so dreaded for a while. It's quite simply the most un-inviting news that I've to share with others, and especially, with my most significant other; who, surprisingly, hasn't come to check on me. And, it's just like John has since said: "'...There's just never a good time to deliver sad or bad news....'" So, I ought to move it—or, deliver such news..., correct.

I'm now standing instead of rising and shining; just, like the reddish-yellow-colored fire-ball in the baby-blue-colored sky of a heaven, or a haven. Move it...! For life goes right on, or rushes on, but not necessarily—up—or, upwards. I'm now up and about, putting on an old house coat of mine.... It usually lies on a chaise near our bed, *Xina's* and mine. Anxiety has well set in!

This is to say, most, definitely, that I just dread having to tell her— *Xina*, the sadly bad news. That I'm now job-less. I'm such after every thing that I've been through with my Uncle Sam and all. After having secured my house coat on my tall, toneful, and naturally tannish body; and, then, having stepped into a pair of my nearby house shoes; I'll be disappearing from the bed room. But, not, before I stop right in front of the dresser's big looking glass, or mirror. See just how quick anxiety and dread or badly sad news is so affecting my being—or spirit—me.

There's no doubt, either, that I've my fair or just share of grey hairs and wide wrinkles, already, at the not so tender age of 40—or, 41; because, both ages are related, or relevant, and roundly. It's almost impossible to ever look good, or great, if one hasn't certain things; and, almost certainly, if such things are almost never forth-coming or long-lasting: real peace, health, love, and happiness, and even success; all of which, almost, always, require, if not demand, rightly, a certain level of commitment, perseverance, and, courage. What about my own self...? I just question the mirror or looking glass. For, I know that it's not about to lie to me or betray me in any way, what so ever.

To some extent, I've almost always possessed such things, courage, perseverance, commitment, success, and so forth. But, now, well, I'm just— not, that goddamn sure.... Secretly, I'm so tired of busting my butt or behind and hustling for another or some other—all, to what damned or actual avail? Huh?

Well, it's been to some avail or advantage, clearly, as life's been good to me, to a great extent. Still, I'm now job-less—Oh God...! MOVE IT! I'm now moving on. Or, I'm disappearing from this room that's almost, certainly, no sanctuary, or safe haven. There's just no escaping or even prolonging the inevitable: Right?

In the very airily bright kitchen, an olive-skinned, and short-sized, yet shapely woman of a lovingly lovely wife and mother...; or, *Xina* Dunbar is getting about the busy business of the morning, busily. She's fixing our big breakfast: the usual; I can smell it all, and, well: some de-caffeinated coffee; some thick ham and cheese omelets; some golden hash browns; some toasty English muffins; all of which are almost certainly ready to be consumed. But, not, before *Xina* tops every thing—right, off, with a very mouth-wateringly colorful fruit salad; whose sweet cantaloupe, honey dew, grapes, kiwis, and pine apples, and even water melon; all of which, probably, won't be enough to sweeten my sadly sour news or bad news—damned dark day.

Still, she's just slicing away or slicing up the so colorfully sweet fruit right into bits and pieces.... Again, will such be enough to put my life right back into a sweetly bright whole? I dare not ask my wife—*Xina*, such, either. I'm now moving right into the kitchen.

What's more, right, beneath my half-frowning, I'm even half-smiling, and moving right on, up, or down, or even round about. Walking around the center counter, I now greet the great love of my life or my wonderful wife: "Mornin' Luv," I say, and just trying hard to project a lightly brave face. Yet, she sees right under or right through it: or, my fantastically ill-fated façade.

Now, doing an about-face, facing me, "What's wrong..., Dear? And, who was that telephoning so damn early?" questions *Xina*.

I answer back, "John, and he was bearing some sad—or, bad news."

"What?"

"I've been let go—"

"OH NO...!"

"Yes, it's so, 'very true.' I now wish, too, that I could've or would've made E-7. Then, just, stayed put right in Uncle Sam's army for another 4 or 6 years. Instead of having so reached high-year tenure at 22-plus years—or, so having been booted out. At least, then, my little or modest pension could've or even would've been a little bit more than 50% or so, of my base pay.... GODDAMIT...!"

Xina tells me, "Settle down, Deary," and pushing aside that brightly sweet-looking fruit-salad.

Moving right toward the refrigerator, I'm in real need of a little or a big poisonous crutch to lean on, for support. Opening it—icebox, where upon my smokes are kept fresh, I just blurt out...: "Right now, I'll have something stiff—or, a shot of cold liquor, or even a warmly refrigerative or refrigeratory smoke—"

"I'll fix you a cup of hot tea—"

"…Fine—but, please, just, make that some hotly caffeinated coffee, instead. Because, round about now, I need as much stimulation as I can get—or, muster," I state. I then get that circularly cool or cold poison of a crutch. Next, I get a book of matches from a drawer.

With my warm house coat, and my warmly comfortable house shoes both right on; I'm now en route right to the house's back patio of a would-be retreat. Needless, to say—that, right now, isn't a good time, most, probably, to retreat—but, instead—just, fight. That's right…! To do such with all of my goddamn might every single damned day and night, forth-rightly!

"My Dear, I'll bring you that coffee…. Also, I must insist—still, that you've a big breakfast—"

"Fine, Luv. For, it too will be needed right along with my other pick-me-uppers. To, send me right on my new job-search so full of solids that are very well stimulated or solidified, 'quite solidly.'"

While exiting the kitchen or the main house, I just can't help blurting right out, rather blusteringly: "…Damn those damned terrorists of September the eleventh…!"

Xina's voice only trails me, "PLEASE, SETTLE DOWN, DEAR…!"

The words ricochet, and, roundly, from my mouth un-intentionally—yet, some-how, consciously, enough: "Settle down? We've bills to pay, Luv, and some that're serious…."

Scene 3

What a lovely and bright sight. I've up-graded our house's scenery, recently. Plus, I'm pleased most particularly by the new back view. I'm now a part of it—view, or, scene. Or rather, it'll brighten with a bit of luck, if not heighten my darkly low spirit…. I'm still talking about the damned sad, and bad, or dark news of John's. It's left me not at all glad but mad. How could I've allowed myself to be had, and, quite?

After I step near one of four patio tables with similar chairs that're on the back patio, I just take a seat, so uncomfortably. Since, my steps have been weighted, unmeasured, and hurried, without doubt, fail. I just need to relieve some of the weight that's currently weighing me right down: It's all about my utterly uncertain or woefully weighty fate….

Fortunately, I can hear, see, smell, and feel, and even taste, already, the poison that's moving right in for the kill. With any luck, it'll slay some of my un-certainty, or anxiety. After lighting my poisonous cigarette…, I settle back, some. Or, I just let the poison do some of the damn settling.

Next, I look all around.... I'm just looking at the colorfully candied colors of ruby-red, olive-green, mellow-yellow, and, pristine-pink, and, even, snow-white. They're the circularly colorful colors of the stretched-out deck and garden—scene, or, setting; whose rocks, grass, bushes, plants, roses, and all, are colored quite beautifully. But, can it all turn my darkly gray day to a brightly gay day, uh? I'm inclined to think not....

Right, after I dump my ashes in the crystal ash-tray that's atop the patio table; I just veer my uncomfortable position in the pretty pillowy seat of cast-iron. I then continue looking around and thinking—that, I'll need nerves of pitch-black steel....

Right, through the very hazy smoke of my nakedly sweet poison, I'm surely seeing some day, or morning. It's begun so sourly, for damn sure. I see such right in the reflection that's so reflecting, and roundly, off the turquoise-colored water of the very near Olympic-sized swimming pool; whose built-in whirlpool's size, and shape, and even dead bubbles, and all, are un-inviting—at best—or worst, threatening.

I want to just burst out! "Sons-of-Bitches...!" I explode, explosively, banging my right and super tight fist on the circular glass of the patio table. Thrillingly, or movingly, if not circularly, it shakes right to a starkly strident shrill—BANG! More, if my left hand hadn't been cuddling my pretty sweet poison, it also would've had a big part in the joyously ugly banging. ...Today has been forth coming. Hasn't it?

...Since the towering terrorism in New York City, on September the 11th, 2001—of this year, my firm's business has been lacking, business. Or, it's been slowing right to an utterly un-acceptable crawl.... Much money has been so lost, even, in my retirement accounts, stocks, bonds, and so on. There are certain lives that just have to be lived; certain bills that just have to be paid; certain futures that just have to be secured; all, to what goddamn avail? Huh?

Finally, I kill my cigarette in the ash tray. Then, I just think to myself. That, I would've even killed those dark, dirty, deranged, and dangerous, and even deathly; or, those damnably terrible terrorists with my own damn naked or bare hands, if ever given the chance. Damnation...! I'll be goddamned if I permit such to just ruin every single, damn, thing.

"DAMNIT...!" I screech, seething, mad. I can't and won't continue being had or dependent on some damned firm of a business; whose business' success, almost, always, rests, and roundly, right, on certain certainties: or, an indefinite influx of the influentially rich and their roundly robust riches.

Scene 4

Having since dressed right in a warmly inviting, flowery, and colorful house-robe, my wonderful wife—or, *Xina* Dunbar is now appearing on the scene. She's stepping lightly, straightly, and forwardly, in a pair of colorfully light and warm and even slightly heeled house-shoes.

"…Please, Deary, just, don't do it…!" pleads *Xina*, nearing my patio table—me.

I can see, clearly, too, that she's in no mood, at all, for any negativity. Approaching my patio table or me, *Xina* continues, so optimistically: "Others may live right in the ditches with or without their riches—but, not you—my Dear." She then places that hotly caffeinated cup of coffee right down, on the table—and, right, in front of me.

"Thank you…, Luv," I say. Plus, I even see that my day has a really round ray of super bright light. That's right. I'm being picked up, mentally, emotionally, and, physically, and, even, spiritually…. Now, such isn't to say, either, that, those other poisonous stimulants of mine haven't lifted my being, up. That, in all probability such has done so, and, duly.

Xina states, "Oh, my Darling…! There's almost never anything that I couldn't or wouldn't do for you…," sitting, down. She does such, or sits right across the table from me while I immediately flavor my coffee. Continuing, on, "Your breakfast's coming up—"

"Yes, I know…."

…She continues with such or much optimism or, an overly optimistic push: "I can't and won't allow anything to get you down—NO SIRREE! Not John or anything else—job lost, impending bills—nothing, at all, should—or, will get you down," *Xina* ends…, somewhat, stammeringly.

I just savor a very long swallow of the poison—or the coffee, which has sat most un-tiredly before me. Afterwards, I look lovingly at my wife of a wonderful woman; whose face radiates hope, ambition, and strength—or sure staying power: *personal power*. I ought to just draw upon those visual if not visceral qualities of hers…. Or, even, I really ought to continue wearing the paternal pants…, correct? Be a super strong man; whose commitment to, and perseverance in, lifting me or us—up, from some deeply and damnably dark ditch just has to be.

I, once again, see, as well as smell, hear, and taste, and even feel the absolute awesomeness of my wife's or *Xina's* spirit, or being; whose wildly wonderful thoughts, words, and ways are even parallel to her very wonderful features; whose somewhat slant and lightly hazel-nut-colored eyes are resting under naturally arched brows; whose arches are centered perfectly above an equally symmetric mouth; whose shinily labored lips envelop a lovely set of pearly-whites or snow-white-colored teeth; all centers so high and wide amid *Xina's* roundly rosy-colored cheeks.

Through the disappointingly and terribly thick cloud of job-less-ness and dark-ness, which has left a starkly dark haze all over me…; and, with a frozenly scary glaze just glazing me, I'm now seeing them: *Xina's* very well-cared-for teeth. She's just smiling lovingly at me, before speaking…: "We've so very much to be thankful for—and, we'll go on being so very thankful—"

"Why sure you're so right," I interpose or interpolate, agreeing with *Xina*, rightfully, and, rather; "After all, we've come a long way—"

"That's right, and, a very long way…! Deary, for we've come all the way from a hole in the wall of a disco. Never again, though!" exclaims *Xina*, so edgily—and, with an exceedingly edgy expression that's right on her face; whose brows are now raised; whose eyes are now pierced; whose nose is now crinkled; whose mouth is now pouted; "Never, ever, again…!" she stresses— or swears, unequivocally, and intolerantly, and even irrevocably.

"Just, settle down…, Luv!" I tell *Xina*. I'm even experiencing her past pain that's never brought her any genuine gain—except, for me—and, for my uncle. That's so correct. Uncle Sam and I both rescued my wife from a life of nothingness, figuratively, and literally.

"…Never again, will I permit my-self to work for some damn golden-colored gold-digger in some damned no-good place on some god-damned no-good piece of a job…. NEVER AGAIN…!" *Xina* reiterates, roundly, and, in-capable of settling down, quite seemingly. It's her utterly un-pretty past that's coming, currently, or right to the front of my soundly stimulant mind. Most definitely, it was a damnably dark time in *Xina's* single life. Such had been the case—well, before she became my irreplaceable wife.

Plus, my pretty poisonous stimulants are just like very sharp knives. That're so stabbing me in all of the wrong places and then in all of the right places. Once more, I'm returning there: To that place, while at the same time, flavoring, if not savoring my semi-stimulative poison—or, now warmed-over coffee.

Act II

Scene 1

Seoul, South Korea

U.S. Army Garrison Yongsan—The Past

On a nakedly dark, yet lucid and sultry and even over-due or un-welcoming night in the late summer of 1980; in a relatively run-down, and a some-what round, yet small room of a discotheque near U.S. Army Garrison *Yongsan*; a racially mixed group of male soldiers have all gathered.

The un-aged, medium-sized, made-up, and *Korean* woman of a boss is standing tall, if not stiffly, at the door of her small office. Such stance, almost, always, affords her both overt and covert opportunities; to monitor, so periodically, or very vigilantly, the comings and goings of her often-times soldierly and disorderly clientele; as well as her employees that're mostly and un-incidentally young, pretty, and shapely females—*Koreans*.

Right, from my vantage point, the psychedelic lights that're flashing above my somewhat secluded table for two, aren't skewing my good view of the real goings-on. What's going on, mainly, is that off-duty soldiers—just, like me, are all just trying to release some hot steam.… It's endlessly steamy pressure that's put upon us soldiers—right, by our Uncle Sam of a definitely demanding presser: pressing production…!

So, we're all right here at Club Cherry, steaming away, or producing. And, not only can I see clearly; but, I can say, also, that a bunch of roundly rowdy soldiers sitting at a particular table are producing or releasing such or much damn steam: drinking too plentifully; smoking too plentifully; talking too plentifully; butt-watching too plentifully; butt-grabbing too licentiously, if not too lecherously, and so forth.

I can see, even, that the boss-woman of a supervisor—or, Mama-Boss is about through just standing back—still. Those rowdy soldiers of drunkenly sexual leeches are most likely too damn touchy-feely for her…; whose very well known job is to protect and even defend the females that're under her supervision, without doubt, or fail.

Once more, she's just about through just standing still—or, back; and, letting those licentious leeches leech off or leech upon her female employees, or female waitresses—servers…; and, some of whom, appearances, manners, and the like, are so sexually suggestive, to say the least. More, some of those female servers are even getting up-close and personal with their customers…, or leeches.

But, those roundly rowdy soldiers are being far too damn personal, if I myself may say so. They're reaching out and touching one female server, in particular—and, quite in-appropriately. I'm talking all about feeling the tight-fitting clothing of the female's butt—or, shapely behind. They're doing such, right, in between her having since brought two pitchers of some seemingly strong, thick, and, dark beer, or, poison; right, to the rowdily or the circularly consumptive males or soldiers, damned leeches.

The female server has had enough, apparently, and, interestingly. The olive-skinned, short-sized, yet shapely, and lovely—or, young woman of a server, slaps the hand—very hard, of one of those rowdy soldiers; who's felt, obviously, that his feely-touchy ways are welcoming, to say the least. More, the female storms off, and, rather steadily, after such: delivering the soldiers' poison to them. What's more, may I add—that, she's not behaving sexually suggestive—none, at all.

Scene 2
Continued

Her manner of dress almost certainly represents the woman's success. Right, in a pair of gold-heeled shoes; and, wearing a gold-colored, pants set; and even, dripping in gold jewelry; the boss-woman is now marching over, if not storming to that table….

She's storming or marching…, rather steadily, right, pass the circular-shaped dance floor; upon which folks are dancing, quite dancingly, or most circularly; whose roundly raised dance floor is accommodating a colorfully, stylishly, and dancingly young disc-jockey, or D.J.; who's been playing the soulfully up-beat sounds of Donna Summer's "Hot Stuff," and even her super sensual sounds of "Love to Love You Baby."

Approaching it—that table of roundly rowdy soldiers—or males, the woman-boss greets them, most unshakably: "Whoa…! And listen up—here," she says—or, demands in an utterly unshakable voice; "Settle down! I know that y'all are just lettin' off some steam or some pressure, but y'all are scarin' a few of my girls. They're nervous—"

"Say what?" questions a light-tan-colored soldier.

"SETTLE DOWN!"

"Ahhh, Man—or, Woman…," gripes another soldier that's dark-tan-colored.

"Now, Mama-Boss, why do you want or need to put the brakes on us? Huh? After all we've been through—or, done—uh…?" the light-tan-colored soldier questions, again.

"Sorry Guys…, but y'all just have to settle down—NOW! Otherwise, well, y'all will be booted right out—"

"All right…," the light-tan-colored soldier just acquiesces, and even puffing, poisonously, on a cigarette—or, a Marlboro, more than likely.

Nor is the pretty poisonous smoke of that cigarette clouding the boss-woman's clarity of vision; carrying on, and strictly, or confidently: "Please, just, know that we don't want or need *the Law*, here—"

"For sure....," comments yet another soldier, or Hispanic male; "since, we've enough problems—already, dealing with Uncle Sam, and all."

"Thank you, Guys. And, y'all have a good night...," ending her little or big reprimand of a down-right demand, (SETTLE DOWN!). The woman-boss even gives the soldiers one last, deafening, and super strict stare-down. She does so—right, before spinning, self-assuredly, on her golden heels and then disappearing from the scene, rather goldenly.

The last two and seemingly subdued if not silent, or male soldiers in the gang now stand up from their messy table, so oddly, enough. Wordlessly, the one Asian soldier just points, unmistakably, at the door or exit. It's where the second Black soldier heads, too, toward the exit, or door, following suit. Indeed, all of the male soldiers end their no longer steamy visit; whose un-welcoming steam or pressure has since been dispelled, some.

This is to say—that, they're all now following suit, as well: finishing their drinking; finishing their smoking; finishing their talking; finishing their butt-watching; finishing their butt-grabbing—here. Yet, it would be an under-statement, so surely: to say, that the males are headed elsewhere, probably; to finish releasing some pressure or some steam; whose steam or pressure has only just begun to be released.

Eventually, that bunch of male soldiers leave this disco of a hot night spot, which I'm my-self about finished visiting; but, not, before I've a little drink or two; or, not, before that olive-skinned, short-sized, yet shapely, and lovely—or, young woman of a server serves me.

She's now coming right toward me, and smilingly, and even fatefully. YIPPEE! That's so right. Tonight, I'm just about to take a great big bite right out of my singleness if not aloneness—and, with all my doggone might. It's been rumored, so roundly, and rather ridiculously: That, if Uncle Sam wanted his employees to be all family-like—then, they would've been issued such, a family. In any case, I'm not about to let such a roundly ridiculous rumor stop me, from my being a wonderfully white knight: or, a beautifully black knight.

Oh, WOW...! What an exceedingly exotic female of a server. Now, she's almost here or near me. And, I'm feeling light, already, as it were. For, I'm no longer weighted way down by aloneness or singleness. That's right—correct! I'll soon have some real height above the doggoned dog-eat-male—fight, that's Uncle Sam's.

At this moment, she's not just in sight. But, that olive-skinned, short-sized, yet shapely, and lovely—young woman, or server is standing right in front of me. She's at my table, smiling, seductively. That she's up close and in person, even. In the end, who'll seduce who, truly? HOOPLA…!

Scene 3
San Diego, California
The Present

Sitting, right, down, "Deary," speaks *Xina*, "DEARY…!" *Xina* blurts out, again. She's even leaning over a big serving tray. It's filled with that big breakfast of ours, (and an accompanied news-paper that I just place aside).

"Oh! Thanks, Luv…," I finally answer back—or, ask: "When did you disappear from the table? I didn't even see you—"

"You're day-dreaming or, so it appeared or seemed to me. Thus, I just moseyed away—"

"Hey!" I exclaim, and just smiling, some; "I can't or won't complain about your disappearance, at all. Since, I'm all ready to eat up or chow down. It's just time for some serious solids to solidify my new will, most solidly, in securing some seriously new employment."

Xina pushes the serving tray and the news paper both, my way—or, in front of me right on the patio table, oddly, enough. She continues speaking—asking: "Although you're sitting right here with me, you weren't really here. So, where were you? Or, what about your day-dream…?"

"I was just reminiscing about my first meeting you at Club Cherry…. How you're so disgusted…, seemingly, or, fed up, actually, with all the butt-watching and butt-grabbing of some roundly rowdy male-soldiers—"

Xina proclaims, "NEVER AGAIN…!" sitting comfortably at the table and is now about to chow down or just eat up. With our respective food-stuff having been placed, roundly, about each other or one another; we'll continue our candor, circularly, with super sweet sayings in the middle of our eating or our dining, outdoors.

"Of course," I continue, and, candidly, "such was especially easy for you to say—never again, once Uncle Sam and I both had rescued you…."

"And, not, a day too goddamn soon…, quite, thankfully," says *Xina*, and biting, right, into her buttery English muffin. Carrying on; "But, I really was seduced way before that. Our eventual friendship, courtship, marriage, family, life, and all, have been a deliciously good, or a heavenly dream come true for me. I thank you, too, particularly, for our wonderful son—"

Now putting the news-paper aside, again, I interpolate: "Yes, let's not forget about that son of ours," for I'm a little worried; "God only knows what Derrick Junior will think or say about my job-less-ness—"

From the outside, she's a little surprised..., and interjecting: "You've been a great father..., and all, which is why you don't want him to see you, down, in the starkly dark ditches. Most brightly, he looks up to you—"

"I know—yet, I'm a little worried, still. There are our family finances and all to consider...," I comment, uncomfortably. I've done so, speaking my true thoughts prior to gulping down a mixture of food.

Xina swallows a very long swallow of her coffee.... Next, *Xina* states her true thoughts, also: "You'll manage just fine. Or, we'll manage just fine. It's what we've done, almost, always—Deary."

"Thanks, Luv, for your utterly un-dying love and support all through the years, or, for the last two decades of my life, or strife. You've been such a lovingly supportive and wonderful wife and even mother."

"I'll just continue to do—or be such, beyond doubt. This is why I now believe that you should just start your *own* business—or, just get a brand new career, life. You're educated, experienced, and entrepreneurial, for sure."

Agape, I almost gag on the food that's in my mouth; yet, I manage to just swallow it.... "What...?" I then question *Xina* with surprise registering, unquestionably, right, on my face; "Now, that's some thought..., Luv," I add right before finishing up my very warmed-over or warmed-way-down coffee; "Where, my Dear, on God's damnably, if not, darkly brownish-green-colored Earth, would I ever get the money—"

"Don't worry..., Deary. Since, God will make a way as always. And, don't look so damn surprised or shocked by my solidly sound suggestion...," *Xina* suggests, or better yet, interpolates. She's even looking quite confident and all.

"Well, I'm almost certainly confident that you mean well, Luv, and, as always."

All through with her own big breakfast..., *Xina* is now ending our big breakfast-date of an early get-together. It's now leaving me feeling optimistic all about the future or our family's future. She's even begun tidying the table, up.

"What do you've planned for this morning, or day?" I query, finishing up, if not tidying up, myself.

Xina answers in the midst of our straightening things right up: "Well, I'll be running a few errands. Then, I'll most likely volunteer for a few hours, as usual, right, at the Women's Shelter.... What about you...?" inserts *Xina*, cross-questioningly.

28

"I'd better check out the Help-Wanted Ads in the news paper. Make some phone calls, and so on, just—in case—"

"Fine…! But, please, keep in mind what I've since suggested or said. That, you should just start anew.…"

"Of course…," I reply. As my wonderful wife is now kissing me on my lips lovingly. She does so, for only a few seconds.

"Now, you go ahead … whilst I finish tidying up or clearing away our breakfast-stuff, right quick."

"Thank you so…, Luv," I reciprocate—or respond, and then grabbing the newspaper that's just lying next to me on a vacant patio chair.

She's now disappearing from the scene while I'm myself getting busy and, rightfully, so. That's right, true. We're a productively fortyish, if not, a circularly candid couple that's on the go. Produce, or just keep producing.…

Scene 4
Later That Afternoon

After having searched the Help-Wanted Ads; plus, net-working with business associates, friends, and the like, via telephone practically all morning—or, day; and, even, after having had a few stiff shots of cold liquor among other things—all, to no actual avail or gain…; Derrick Dwight Dunbar Senior has ended up—since, right, where his day or morning began. Derrick is just lying on his king-sized bed at his sizeable home on the outskirts of San Diego— right, in the dark master-bedroom suite.

Fatefully, that olive-skinned, short-sized, yet shapely, and lovely; or, young woman of a server isn't just standing right in front of me…, smiling, and seductively, or seemingly. But, she's now asking to serve me or take my order. YIPPEE!

"Hi, and what'll it be?"

"Hi," I respond with an invitingly seductive smile of my own; "and, I'll have something light and smooth and not too 'damn' sweet—"

"What about a Michelob, if I may suggest—"

"Fine," I agree, and, overly; "as I totally trust your suggestion and all. By the way, I apologize for those 'damned, or' roundly rowdy soldiers—"

"Thanks. But, I've since let them go or have forgotten all about those licentiously ill-mannered males."

I just insert and not so innocently yet sincerely and self-servingly but cautiously: "I'd like to make it up to you—for them, if I may? By askin' you out to dinner, properly—a proper date, that is—'Lovely Lady.'"

Seductively, she's smiling, or smirking, or even grinning, outwardly, before speaking: "Why not...? I'm *Xina* and you're...?"

"Oh! Sorry. I'm Derrick Dunbar, and I'm so 'damn' pleased to meet you, *Xina*—"

"The same here—and, let me get your drink—or, beer, before Mama-Boss or Big Bad Bozo goes off. I'll just slip you my phone number, when I get back—"

"That's cool 'or GREAT...!'" I say and am only, too, goddamn happy. We'll go on, as well—both *Xina* and I—to become very good friends: date—court; marry—build a life; have a child; travel world-wide; get educated both worldly and academically; prepare for the future—our real retirement; live a good life, and so forth—produce. Such production will be constructed in the course of two delectable and not so delectable decades.

Act III

Scene 1

Continued

DINNG...! I'll be damned...! Why in the hell is this scene familiar, and, fantastically? DINNNG...! Abruptly, I've been awoken, startlingly, yet consciously, enough, from a restlessly yet damn good day-dream. I'm where? Or better, where I've been? Day dreaming, apparently, right, about our life's journey—*Xina's* and mine.

For sure, it's taken us right on some trip—our life, to say the least...: journeying here, there, and everywhere. That's since brought me right back to where our, or, better, yet, where my latest journey so began.... But, how, exactly, will it all end...? I'm still talking all about, or rather, worrying all about my job-less-ness. That's right! I've some fight ahead of me: DINNNG! I snatch the telephone from the bed stand that's aside of me, so reluctantly, yet bravely, and anxiously.

Good...! From else where in the house, *Xina's* voice will sound right out. It'll drown right out my invisibly silent interception of her telephonic conversation. That's correct; I'll only listen to the two: or, one being the great love of my love-life; and, the other being the great pride of my life: "Hello," answers *Xina*.

"Hello Mother," speaks Derrick Junior in a curiously anxious, if not a curiously eager voice; "I've since gotten your voice message—"

"Hello Sweetie or, my Darling Son. Yes, I called you...," states *Xina* with an out-of-breath and hushful voice; "it's your father—and, he may very well be starting a spanking brand new life—career—"

"Oh?"

"Yes, if I've my way and I intend to—"

"Mother, what're you talking about?"

"He's since been let go, from that super slave-driving job—"

"What? Oh no...!" Derrick asks—then, exclaims, with a little raised voice.

"It's the recession and all. Now is your father's time. He needs to just spread his entrepreneurial wings and then fly high—or, soar. Just, strike right out—and, right now...!"

"I love Dad and will support or help him, in any way, what so ever," Derrick tells *Xina* quite lovingly and most supportingly.

"I know—and, well, there's our monetary matter to consider and all. Lately, we've lost some money—"

"I reckon so...," says Derrick Junior; "since folks have been hit hard, financially—that is. The stock market has gone way down and so on."

"Yes, indeed," *Xina* concurs, if not fearful, furtively; "which is why we ought to just travel a more financially independent road from here—out!"

"I agree whole-heartedly, Mother. And, naturally, I'm always here for you—or him, Dad."

"Thank you, Sweetie, and now I should go. I just got in after having been so out and about. Dinner needs fixing and all. Also, I'm un-sure of your father's whereabouts—"

"How's he doing...?" questions Derrick Junior, with a now hushed or low voice of his very own.

"Well, your father's been busy, and, really, busying him-self with his new job-search, and all."

"Don't worry, Mother, for things will work out—"

"Of course," *Xina* interpolates, "you're so right..., especially, if I've my way, which I intend to."

Some silence ensues—but, only, for a few seconds or so.... Then, the two just end their not so secretive, telephonic conversation: "We'll talk later, Sweetie—"

"All right, Mother—and, bye-bye."

"Bye."

Bless Derrick Dwight Dunbar Junior or our super sweet son, *Xina's* and mine. I now dis-engage right from the telephone—but, only, after *Xina's* disengagement or disconnection...: GREAT! Apparently, the two didn't even discover my silently invisible interception or hush-hush intrusion. It's just as well, too, for the two—mother and son—would've been so bound, anyway, to have such talk, or pep-talk, some-how.

Scene 2
Continued

...Crawling back whence I've so lain, and restlessly, for the latter part of the day—right, on the bed...; I'm now feeling more comfortable—or, so restful, actually. That's right. I've a fantastically funny feeling that things are going to turn around or work out well, for me. My some-what successful son will help me, some-way. Now, I'm lying back comfortably on the king-sized bed. Luckily, anxiety isn't setting in.

Still, I'm so envisioning the past and the present and even the future. They're joined together and forever—right, on a bed of uncertainty imbued with even more uncertainty. I'm certain, however, that I should just go right with the flow, or flood. In other words—most likely, now isn't the time, for me to back-slide into a slimily pitch-black sea of conscious or un-conscious in-consistency.

Some pretty persistent indulgence is required, here. As, it's what I've almost always instilled in my son among some other things...: morality, and ethics, and even character. Having moral values or a serious set of principles to live by; whose methodologies or methods are right and motives—good, is, of great consequence. It's even giving me some wonderfully warm comfort, knowing such. That, I've done right by Derrick Junior and will continue to be good....

I've to just obtain a new j-o-b, or career. Moreover, try to retain if not maintain some super steady standards just like my son. Thank goodness, too! That, Derrick Junior hasn't turned right out to be a damned army-brat. But, instead, he's turned out to be a young man of some substance, or character; who's since worked his way right through college, having majored, dually, in accounting, and economics.

I've my-self a college degree in business administration with a minor in management. Put it to some damn good use, then: Now! Though, how so is the zillion-dollar-question? Should I start a security business of some sort...? I've some professional and social and even personal contacts.... Good! *Xina* could help right with her college degree in English and all. She'd be a great administrator or an administrative assistant. In addition, to her being, already, a productively hard-working house-wife.

However, I shouldn't expect Derrick Junior to join me and all. He has a full-time job, already, as an up-and-coming accountant at Astir Accounting Services. Oh! Boy! Does that boy of mine like balancing financial figures or financial numbers. He's been a super smart investor, to boot. That's correct. Derrick Junior has chosen to put the bulk of his hard-earned if not hard-won money in commodities, precious metals, and bonds, and even real estate.

Why didn't we or *Xina* and I both just follow his suit? Sure, Derrick Junior has made some hard cash in the stock market…. Yet, he was gradually skeptical of, and even spooked, seriously, by its resplendently robust rise…. Derrick Junior even chose to invest, and wisely, the educational fund—or, money; which *Xina* and I both had saved for him…; instead, having chosen a slew of academic scholarships, grants, and full-time jobs, and even part-time jobs—only, to pay for college. He's some son, right? Feeling comfortable—that, that boy of mine is doing just fine, I continue lying back comfortably.

A great big smile of a smirk just can't help popping right on my face. I'm only too damn smitten by my son's success. Truthfully, it's an on-going process or successive or even progressive quest to be the best at living this thing called life. My wife and I both know all about it…. Good! That Derrick Junior is progressing, and personally—or even, dating. He'll be ready to have a lovingly supportive family of his very own, soon: GREAT!

Until then, Derrick Junior has been and will just continue to be quite loving and supportive of us, or *Xina* and me, right, in most of our endeavors. Needless, to say, that Derrick Junior was very disturbed—at best—or worst, down-right dis-pleased. When, *Xina* and I both had told him all about our gigantic, financial strategy. To capitalize, circularly, if not fabulously, on the stock market some years ago: its staggeringly—or, its roundly robust rise.

…Why didn't I get out of the stock market—right, before it crumbled into some very un-pretty pieces…? Such spendable hope, and faith, and even ambition—or greed—plain, and simple, has since caused my present loss or losses. BOO, HOO…! Never again, though. Since, I'm now seeing that super son of mine right inside a wildly bright corner of my mind.

He's just carrying on, so smartly, and strongly, and even successfully, after that somewhat secretly telephonic conversation of his and *Xina's*. That's right. For, I know of not only my son's methodologies by which he lives life, but also his philosophical principles of living it, life. Or better, I just can't help drifting right off, subconsciously, and, rather comfortably: Knowing that Derrick Junior is very much keeping his word, or honor, right, to his mother, especially: saying that things will work out….

Having since worked out or exercised intensely instead of extensively; in the very well-resourced gym of his totally trendy town-house; in the so colorfully cosmopolitan area of San Diego, California; Derrick Junior is now relaxing, some; right, before he telephones his certified financial planner (*C.F.P.*)...: or, his moneyed manager of a moneyed wizard; on a late afternoon that is fast becoming a fruitfully bright evening or night.

That's right—correct! He's some generously light-chocolate-colored knight that's so dressed in an athletically off-white-colored pants suit. Whilst sitting back on the black, leathern, and sectional settee in the living room...; Derrick Junior wipes the little perspiration from his silk-like face...; which, almost, certainly, radiates some inspiration amid some fine-looking features: well-shaped brows; slant yet bright light-brown eyes; pretty pint-sized nose; plus, lip-smacking lips. He's done so—or, so wiped his face, while flavoring, simultaneously, something sparkly, perhaps, some spark-like water. Having relaxed, some, it's now time for Derrick Junior to carry on, smartly, strongly, and successfully, of course; and, just, as he's done so often in the past when confronted right with the present or even the future.

Presently, he's placing that fancy glass of bubbly liquid down—right, on a very leathery coaster atop the centered coffee table; whose speckled and gray-colored marble is shimmering beneath the living room's lighting that's so recessed, and roundly.

While putting down that nearly through and naturally athletic drink of his, Derrick Junior even checks the time of his *Movado*, watch. It's reading nine o'clock, sharp. And, without doubt, time is of some essence, here. Since, it has the true power to permeate the past and the present and even the future: A future and present and even past that're fast becoming one of the same.

Now, he's up and about, moving with some speed in a pair of utterly up-to-the-minute-looking sneakers. Derrick Junior is even heading toward a technologically advanced-looking telephone that's on an end table of sort.

He just pushes down some button or another button on the telephone. It then starts dialing some telephonic number or another telephonic number.

"Hello," a very business-like voice answers out..., on the telephone's speaker-phone.

"Hi Mike," speaks Derrick Junior, in his normal tone of voice, now; and, quite, un-like that hush-hush voice of his, earlier...; "it's Derrick and I really need to entangle myself from an existent jam—"

"Oh?"

"Indeed," says Derrick, and shifting his muscularly sculturesque if not statuesque stance; whose medium-sized frame, and all, almost, never, sway, under any pressure whether unpropitious or not.

…Mr. Mike Mason then asks, or—better yet, splutters—and, almost, apologetically…: "What do you need—or, want…? Or, what can I do—" his questions being answered, rather abruptly.

"$50, 000," Derrick Junior blurts out, right quick.

"When…?"

"*ASAP*—or, as soon as possible…! Oh! And, that'll be a certified cashier's check made out to my father, or Derrick Dwight Dunbar Senior."

"Very well," Mike acknowledges the request or polite demand; "I'll get back with you…, soon. Also, Derrick, I'm hoping that all is all right—or, isn't it?" Mike queries, or, pries, some.

"No, it isn't…," states Derrick Junior in a steady if not a stony voice; "but, that's all changing, now, beginning right with my $50,000—gift, to my father. He has to start anew—"

"I see—or, understand," Mike comments—and then asks—"it's the economy or the lack there of—right?"

"That's correct, right."

"Yes, un-fortunately, and currently, I've some associates that're way down at their very own heels…."

"…Businesses, employees, clients—or, everybody's just suffering—and, mainly, because of September the 11th—goddamned terrorists…!"

"To be damn sure, and—well, let me get started or get right to work," Mike tells Derrick Junior.

"Okay. And, thanks, Mike, for everything. I'm sorry about my timing, too."

"It's my pleasure, or my privilege…, Derrick, and I'll be in touch—very, soon. Good-bye now."

"Good-by," Derrick Junior now ends his conversation or even request of a pretty, damn polite demand.

Next, he twirls on his thickly rubber heels. Derrick Junior is heading for the super spacious stairs that're leading up-stairs. There, most likely, he'll indulge a steamily hot shower in the wonderfully well-appointed master-rest-room of his; whose tint-like glass probable won't screen all the steam; which, almost, certainly, will stream right from the technically advanced shower's gadgets, and all; that're right in the shower of a glass stall; all of which, just, makes me want to scream out this deliciously good dream, or day-dream, as it were.

That very young or twenty-something son of mine—Derrick Junior, has sure done well for himself. Hasn't he gotten sort of a hot lot in life? Or, hasn't he done away with some rot, or decay, already? Yes! Without a doubt, I do believe so.

At this second, I even know that my decidedly delicious day-dream is being lowered…, or even disappearing—right, in reality. Since, I'm hearing some other distinct noise.

Scene 4

It's the door of our bedroom having been opened by *Xina*, smilingly, and lovingly, yet squeakily. I forgot to spray the door's damned hinges with some lubricant, or WD-40. Opening my eyes…, I now see right through the bedroom's lamp's ultra-low lighting. It's just the darkly sweet sight of my wonderfully loving and supportive wife. She's coming right toward our love-full bed—or, me; what about it being sex-full or otherwise?

"Hi Sexy," I purr, with absolute anticipation.…

…Wearing a sexily pearl-colored, sheath-styled, form-fitted, and mid-length, and even cost-effective dress—*Xina* nears me.

Then, right, out of the deep dark blue, she spins sideward—or, away. That's right. The great love of my life or, my super sexy wife has just cut me down with an uninvitingly big knife: OUCH…! Utterly taken aback and then forward, I question, curiously, if not, disappointedly, yet, almost certainly—lovingly, and, forgivingly: "Where you're headed, Luv? I thought that you're going to join me. To cuddle up, or even coddle down, on top of the bed—for, some lovely merry-making—or, some merry love-making…, 'to make merry, merrier, if not the merriest.'"

"Sorry, Dear, and I was going to get off of my feet, some. Since, I've been on that doggedly heated beat of a very hot seat…," *Xina* explains, and walking right into her personal closet. There, she's getting comfortable, most, presumably. Continuing, right, on…; "Traffic seemed extra heavy, today, and even heavier at the Women's Shelter. There was simply no sitting down…, at all, today," states *Xina*. She then leaves her circularly commodious closet that senses so automatically one's body heat; which, in return, turns on, and then turns off the closet's lighting.… As you would expect, such lighting has been Derrick Junior's super sensational suggestion, solely.

…*Xina* is now wearing a silkily charcoal-colored Kimono. She's even stepping, steadily, toward our love-lorn bed; whose impatient bed-warmer of a lovingly understandable husband—or, a good-naturedly eager lover is just lying back—still.

"There'll be plenty time for us to just make love or indulge the art of eroticism, my Dear. Right now, though, our dinner is calling out our names, and, so loudly. That is, it takes food to keep up the damn fight. Or, to give us some brand spanking new might for the damned fight, right?" *Xina* asks—or, better yet, interpolates, and winking, so smilingly, yet powerfully.

That's correct. While explaining her thoughts and actions or the lack there of, very briefly; *Xina* has managed, too, to plant some pretty powerful, or some super sweet kisses right on my face…: to sweeten me right up. "Rise and shine…, Deary," *Xina* adds, if not insists—right, before ending her pretty pep talk, or, her utter uncoupling of us.

"Say what?" I just question and then respond, matter-of-factly, if not deviously; "It's almost time to go to bed or retire and rest, Luv—"

"True, but, until then, you've to rise and shine—still, my Dear," says *Xina*, so smartly, and sternly; "to eat for the heated feat that awaits you on the beat, quite undoubtedly," bouncing up, rather winningly.

"All right, so you've won this round…, Luv. Even so, I intend to win the next one that'll transpire when we're back in bed—"

"Ha-Ha-Ha…!" *Xina* laughs, most affectedly, while stepping away, or sashaying, if not swaggering in a pair of charcoal-colored house-slippers; "So true, too, that good—or rather—great things, almost, always, come to those who wait—"

"Yes, but…, almost, never, come to those who wait too 'goddamn' late or too 'goddamn' long"—I insert, almost insidiously, if not purposefully, and most certainly—affectedly.

She's since disappeared…, or my loving, supportive, wonderful, and sexy, and even understandably demanding wife—*Xina*.

Up, and about, I'm now dressing, so casually, in a pretty plain short-set of sort; having since dis-robed right from that deliciously good dream of a day-dream; plus, having since failed, so fantastically, or miserably, to disrobe my brainy and brawny and even sexy wife. I've some life…, right?

No sooner than I step into my house shoes, that I'm out the door of a sex-less bed-room. Ha! I laugh, to my-self, as that'll change—yet, not nearly, soon—enough. Ha-Ha!

Act IV

Scene 1

2 Days Later, Saturday

…On a very early, dry, or clear, and inviting, and even sensationally sunny, Saturday morning, or day; *Xina* Dunbar has risen, extra, early, as usual, to pacify her already damp, colorful, and beloved baby of a front garden; whose white, pink, yellow, and red roses, and even carnations, and all, typically, are not thirsty; yet, will be quenched wateringly—anyway, right, by *Xina*; who is suspicious of her own front yard's irrigation system, quite seemingly.

Moving round and about it, or the irrigation system that's just situated around the circularly wide driveway; *Xina* isn't just fumbling with its widgets and all. But, she's actually tightening loose things right up: or, so it appears to me right from my vantage point.

I'm just looking at her right through the picture window of the living room. As *Xina* would expect, I'm up and about—early, to continue perfecting my business plan; whose components are slowly but surely coming together in a business-like manner.

That's right! I've since managed to put my vision of my prospective, business venture down, on paper. It consists, so chiefly, of my staying right in the security industry as a security analyst, and analyzing other businesses' security, challenges: assets, liabilities, threats, and the like. It was what I also did in Uncle Sam's military world: Analyzed both domestic and international security, threats; just, like the circularly congenital challenges in management information systems (or *M.I.S.*), to say the very least.

I just want or need to get and then keep some lucratively long-lasting contracts with some roundly reputable firms, or businesses, people. Although I've been exposed to such…, already; I just can't and won't jeopardize my reputation—or, good name, by being unethical, immoral, or otherwise. Or, by my committing any sort of graft. I'll simply start anew. Build up a spanking brand new base of clients. I'll do so, too, ambitiously, yet cautiously, or, with certain care.

Nice and slow will be the way to go…, quite, simply. Because, I don't want things to fall down or fall to pieces just as they're being built up. My lovingly supportive wife—*Xina,* has given me some good if not some great in-put or business pointers, even; all of which has been rather welcoming, or very much appreciated…. I'm almost certain, as well, that *Xina's* gratefully gorgeous garden of a baby can't be any more grateful or appreciative than it's already—or can it?

Having since gotten the water hose, she's now sprinkling some water, most lovingly, on that beautifully bright baby of hers—garden, so needless to say. After having done something or another with, or, to the gadgets of the irrigation system, she's doing its job, still, and industriously. Then, *Xina* just stops all of a sudden.... Since, a luxurious-looking and bright-auburn-colored *Audi* is rolling right round the driveway. It's my son's automobile.

Likewise, it's so very interesting, that Derrick Junior doesn't visit his mother—or, us, normally, this early, on any morning. And, early it is, nearing eight o'clock on a sensational Saturday, morning. I even sense that something is going to give way, today. Per, chance, is Derrick Junior bearing something quite propitiously: a brand spanking new business thought of sort; or, a classy client referral; or, even, something else that's pretty propitious or bodes well?

After having glanced at the big clock on the living room's wall, for a second time, I'm now returning my eyes to the two: one is the great love of my live; and, the other is the great pride of my life. They've since greeted, hugging, and kissing. But, what's the two now talking about or discussing? *Xina's* since cast aside her gardening, for the time being; right, whilst she and Derrick Junior both discuss or talk about something or another, seriously. I'm just observing their super stiff stances, stilted expressions, and so on.... Well, I'd better get right on with the morning, or the business of starting my own business and its super serious dogma.

Surely, my son, or Derrick Junior will've questions and some that're somber. Move it, DOGGONIT! I demand—or better, command my dogged-tired feet.... They're moving too doggone slow..., or reluctantly, if not half-heartedly, for me. Never mind—that, they're only sensing what my mind, heart, and body, and even spirit—all, want: to remain, doggedly, right, at the big picture window.... However, since *fate waits upon no one*, I'm presently moving on, or right along or even up, as it were. That's correct or right; I'm so up to the doggedly dark fight...: or, the dog-goned, dog-eat-male fight of a business. Ha! Ha! Ha!

Scene 2

This fantastic scene is fantastically familiar, most seemingly. Just two days ago, to be exact, I'd greeted the great love of my life—or, my wonderful wife—*Xina*: a circularly and a colorfully charismatic cook, cooking; or, more precisely, her having cooked our big breakfast; which, so filled me—up, with solid hope, faith, and ambition, and even strength—or, some staying power: *personal power*. That's right. Prior to having those golden hash browns; thick ham and cheese omelets; toasty English muffins; plus, mouth-watering fruit salad, I just wanted to indulge a little poisonous crutch to lean on for support. Right, after, I'd gotten that sadly bad news from my supervisor, or Deputy Security Officer John Downs about my job-less-ness: Remember?

Then, I'd specifically wanted something stiff or stiffly supportive: a shot of cold liquor or a warm smoke. Yet, *Xina* insisted upon just fixing me a cup of hot tea. But, I settled, so ultimately, on some highly caffeinated coffee and some poisonously sweet smoke, both.

Also, just, as then, with my warm house-robe, and my warm house-shoes—both, on; I'm now en route right to the house's back patio of a retreat, refuge. This time, though, I'm feeling very confident, and, comfortably. With light, short, and slow steps, I'm approaching the same table as then. Yet, I'll be sitting down confidently and comfortably. I'm even trusting in my brand new date with fate; that, I most likely don't or won't have to wait, any longer.

It's just so great! Nor does my magnificent mate or *Xina* have to wait, any longer, or just lie as bait for some utterly un-desirous fate. She and I both used to just hate to wait..., at any rate. Good...! Such days are over, and ostensibly, or obviously. Or rather, there'll be no more extra weight on my plate of life; weighing me right down to a nakedly, if not a damnably dark, hard, cold, and dirty, and even shaky ground, so floundering, right, around. Incidentally, I've since fired it up. Or, I continue to puff on my poisonously sweet smoke; and, not, because it's needed—but, instead, because it's wanted unworriedly—or, unperturbedly.

That's correct. I'm un-worried, currently, or—at ease, even, if things are about to be shaken, about: or, up, down, sideward, around, and, seriously. Does Derrick Junior have some serious questions for me...; if so, to what extent...; and, to what avail...? Or, more, to the point, what exactly should I reveal to him (and even *Xina*): the truth about every single thing? Indeed, for this isn't the time to deceive anyone. My having, almost, always, led that boy of mine so straight, or forwardly, in the wonderfully wicked thoughts, words, and ways of the world.

I just dump the ashes of the sweetly poisonous stick in the ash tray that's right on the patio table. In fact, I'm about ready to just extinguish it, altogether. Since, I so sense that my wife and my son both will join me very soon, here—or, outdoors, on the back patio of a pool deck. My ways, words, and thoughts—all, ought to be very free and very clear of any cloudiness and smokiness, or uncertainty. So, I go right ahead and stub out that darkly sweet poison of mine. Do so, before it snuffs me right off of life's utterly ultra-fine line; which leads right to its gloriously golden gold mine.... It's my time..., right?

Scene 3

For darn sure, there are certainly cottony or candied or even celestial clouds in the colorfully cobalt-colored sky; which, surrounds, circularly, the roundly reddish-orange-colored sun; whose early, and small, and light rays of super sweet sun-light already portends a momentous measure of mellifluous might. That's so right! It appears that today is starting right mightily—or, all right, and, quite.

Now veering my sitting position, some, in the comfortably pillowy yet steely seat of mine, I'm too feeling mighty and rightfully so. Since, I've maintained slow yet steady and safe or sure faith in "the good": my over-all life; wonderful wife; extra nice son; strife of a tight fight, and the like. I even intend to take my biggest damn bite—yet. To do such—right out, of the fake Dark and White Knight's own bitter-sweet fight, or crumbly cup-cake of life.

That is, I aim, so absolutely, to think, and speak, and even conduct the whole truth; or, to just shame him: or, the starkly and damnably dark Devil, Himself, and all that He represents. It's what I've almost always taught that sagaciously sin-less son of mine; who, at present, is joining me on the back patio. It's where I've sat, silently, if not eagerly, in anticipation of my new-fangled fate; which is almost certainly clothed so circularly with good-ness—right? Could it be—that, that deliciously or decidedly good day-dream ... is coming right to life?

He's some generously light-chocolate-colored and very real knight, or Derrick Dwight Dunbar Junior. He's now right in front of me, and, smiling, lovingly, or rather supportingly—without doubt—or fail.

"Good morning, Dad," speaks Derrick Junior, "and, how're you?" He then sits right down—across, from me in an equally pillowy yet steely seat.

"Good morning, Son. And, I'm fine and you…?" I answer and then cross-question.

"I've been all right or, okay. Listen Dad, you're very surprised, most probably, by my extra early visit. But, I didn't want another minute, or hour, or even day to pass right by without my showing up. To support both you and *Xina*, personally, through this latest ordeal of yours or you-all's—"

"Listen Son—and, it's so true that I'm now job-less. Yet, I'm right on track to change all of that. So, please, don't worry—"

"Oh! I'm not at all worried. Since, I know, first-hand, all about your wonderful, work or working ethic. Perceive and believe and then achieve…, without doubt or fail!"

A smile, a grin, or a smirk pops right on my face. For, I'm so smitten by his ability, to almost, always, think, speak, and do the right things…. "So very true," I just comment, and comfortably, or quite proudly. I'm certainly comfortable knowing that Derrick Dunbar Junior absolutely appreciates my philosophy of life, and the methodology by which I live it. Or, how, I've thus lived it—life, right, with all of its damn strife.

41

"Anyway, I've something very special for you, and, *Xina*. It's just a little something…. To show my absolute appreciation, and absolutely, for all that you-all have ever given to me or done for me. Also, please, accept it, as a gift, if you wish, or however you may think most appropriate."

"What is it…, Son?" I question, eagerly, or, quite curiously, with my expression—no doubt, appearing, very circularly, curious. I even sit up right, giving my son my absolute attention: mentally, emotionally, and physically, and even spiritually.

"Well," says Derrick Junior, "it's just a little check for $50,000…, to help you start anew. Or, to just begin your *own* new business that awaits you. Mom and I've since talked about it. I believe, as well, that it's a great way for you to just go from here, out! We even spoke, very briefly, about such upon my arrival, this morning—"

"Oh…," I remark, reservedly. Since, I'd indeed seen the two not that long ago…. They're embroiled right in some seemingly serious sayings, or conversation. Surely, you re-call it—such. Continuing, on, "It's been right on my mind, very truthfully," I admit or confess, "and having seen you and your mother near the driveway. You-all were talking about something or another, seriously."

"Don't worry, Dad, please! We're only discussing how best to present the gift to you. Then, I just decided that I'd to do so, simply—"

"Thank you, Son, from the very bottom of my very grateful heart, or soul…!" I exclaim, very emotionally, with the biggest smile—ever, beaming, widely, on my face; whose features exhibit emotion, rather, unquestionably: brows raised, roundly; eyes opened, overly; nose puckered, prettily; mouth, well, searching for some more absolutely appreciative words to just say, still: "I'm just word-less, Son, or over the moon—ecstatic, quite frankly, to say the very least!" Now, that decidedly or deliciously good dream … is alive, and, well…!

"Dad," Derrick Junior, tells me, "you needn't say anything—except, that you'll now pursue your *own* entrepreneurial endeavor. Fly and then soar heartily, or dynamically, with great gusto! Know, also, that another $50,000 or so is yours, if need be…," and handing me the certified cashier's check.

"Thank you and I promise to do exactly that…! Indeed, I'll pursue my deliciously or my decidedly good dream…! Execute my soon-to-be business or plan…, pretty, productively, without doubt, or fail. Produce…! Thanks so very much…, Son! Plus, I promise to make you and *Xina* both, damn, proud! Or, just, continue to set some sort of example…. 'Or, really wear my pretty paternal pants around, here…!'"

He's now standing up. Derrick Junior has risen to shake my hand…, man-to-man. We do so, too, after I rise whence I've sat, comfortably. More, I've sat most comfortably after having ascertained that, that fine boy of mine

42

isn't about to imagine, say, or do anything, at all: to darken my beautifully bright morning of a delectable day. Remember my just wondering, if not my just worrying about Derrick Junior's possible questioning…?

We're hugging, presently, after having shook hands, firmly, or man-to-man. "I love you so, Son, and you'll forever be the great pride of my life!" I proclaim, or exclaim, quite exuberantly.

"I love you, likewise, Dad," reciprocates Derrick Junior, and roundly, whilst in the midst of our lovingly manly embrace. I even embrace and then kiss my marvelously moneyed gift of a very fat check, and, most gratefully: Whoopla! Or, BALLYHOO…!

The Finale
Scene 4

The great love of my life, or my wonderfully supportive wife—*Xina,* so intuitively, is joining us—Derrick Junior and me—outdoors. Well, maybe, I've spoken far too soon…; as, she's now carrying our remote telephone for some reason or another reason.

She's wearing, too, the same multi-colored, mid-length, and short-set, as earlier. When, she and Derrick Junior both were discussing, and seriously, how best to present me with the most generous gift of a personal and family investment. Interestingly, her steps are strained, some; her posture is stilted, some; and, her expression is stressed, some; in fact, her carriage, or manner of stepping—whole being, is worrisome, some.

…Derrick Junior and I both have dis-engaged—since, right, from our lovingly big embrace. Taken aback, some, we both are just watching as *Xina* approaches us, on the double. She's looking strangely, or un-comfortably, or even un-characteristically, at us—or, at me, more precisely.

Now, her tone of speech or dim dialogue will even worry me, some: "My Dear, Derrick," states *Xina*, "John's called…," handing me the remote telephone, and, some-what, reluctantly; "pretty, please, Deary," she whispers to me, some-what, "stand your god-damn ground since you're just so bound to succeed…."

I take the telephone from her and then sit right down. For, God only knows what old or new news that John will deliver to me this morning, or today. *Xina* and Derrick Junior both just step aside, so curiously: Their brows are now raised; their eyes are now squinted; their noses are now furrowed; plus, their mouths are now so wide opened, as though they now want to say something, rather, conceivably: Like, don't get wound up; or, don't let your damn guard down—and, quite, certainly—not, in this round; or, even, don't be a super silly—dark clown; which is to say, that, I mustn't let indecision so hound me, all around. Or, find me dithering about, most indecisively. There's just no need to see-saw or zig-zag or even wig-wag.

Sitting uncomfortably, at first, and then sitting comfortably, secondly; I just take a deep breath before speaking, soundly: "Good morning, John, and how're you doing...?" and laying down my spanking brand new money of a check.

"Good morning, Derrick, and I'm just fine. What about you...?" he answers—then, cross-questions.

I answer up, and, roundly, "Actually, John, I'm feeling quite good.... Because, the world is mine to conquer..., 'still.' That, I've since gotten right through the bad to get right to what's good—or, great!"

"Well, Derrick, I'm just so amazed by your amazing, if not amazingly new attitude or even marvelous mood that's so up, and, way...! Considering how things have been up, down, and all—"

"That's old news...!" I interpose, and am curious concerning John's telephone call; "so, what's up 'or down...,' John?" I ask, and am just, about, through skirting some issue or the lack thereof.

"Well, Derrick, I may've a darn good job-contact for you—"

"Oh?"

"That's right," says John, whose voice sounds extraordinarily light or polite; "it's an old colleague of mine that's transferring overseas. His position of a security analyst is opening up, and there's a very good chance that it can be yours—"

"Thanks, John—but, truthfully, I'll be striking right out on my own," I inform him, rightfully, and mightily.

An elongated pause ensues before John responds—and, simply, yet, in amazement—almost certainly: "Oh?"

"That's right. I aim, absolutely, to spread my entrepreneurial wings— 'or just fly high, or even soar—right, to my own brand new success.' Still, I so thank you, John, yet again, for every single thing...," I say. I then see the widely sweet smiles on *Xina's* and Derrick Junior's faces—both. Such super sweet smiles if not super secret smirks give me such or much hope, faith, and ambition, and even strength, or *personal power*: so rightly, to just carry on, smartly, strongly, and successfully; "Also, John, we'll talk some more when I see you on Monday morning at the office. At which time, I'll check out..., officially," I add, and smiling or smirking if not grinning openly.

"Well, in that case—very well. Basically, Derrick, I'm speechless—or, taken aback—forward, by your utterly or unsuspectingly new news…!"

"Yeah, I can sure picture that, John. But, life's just so full of utterly unsuspecting twists and turns, and, so particularly, if one just perseveres right through and just commit to it—life, 'without doubt or fail, restraint.'" I state. I then look right at my caringly loving wife; whose son is equally loving and caring of me. …I'm just thinking about that $50,000, of a very generous gift; which is just lying on the patio table, generously, if not goldenly, and almost certainly, gloriously.

"Well, Derrick," says John, wisely, "no one could or should fault you for pursuing your good dreams—or, full potential. My very good friend, do seek a most sincere measure of lasting peace, health, love, and happiness, and even success, or self-fulfillment, or even self-discovery."

"Thank you very much…, John. Likewise, I wish you and yours well as well as a great day—and, all the days there after."

John remarks, nicely, and, quite, "The very same to you, Derrick, or the very soon-to-be entrepreneur. And, good-bye, for now."

We both end our conversation…, lightly, and laughingly. Yet, there's absolutely nothing laughable—at all, about my plan to out-think, out-work, and out-do—all. That would stand in the way of it: my big business plan for success.

After I dis-connect from John, I just put the remote telephone aside or atop the patio table. I then return my full attention right to the two, who're standing right before me: one is the great love of my life; and, the other is the great pride of my life.

I just blurt out, a wee-bit, boastfully, "I'd like to go over my great big business plan with you two…. I trust, too, that it won't be a disappointment. But, instead, will bring *me* end-less employment, specially. And, will bring each of us if not all of us, eventually, some end-less enjoyment, collectively, or especially."

Xina comments, cheerfully, or, rather gleefully, "You've done it, my Dear! By taking a very necessary, first step. You've since let go or cut your damned losses and is now moving on—up!"

Spontaneously, and enthusiastically, and even mightily, I grab hold of my very wonderful wife, and lifting her right up. We kiss keenly and then hug heartily—or, we just hold each other, most lovingly. Then, we just smile at one another, and, smiling, most particularly, at *Xina's* right slipper; that's since slipped right off of her right foot amid our utterly up-lifting embrace of a wonderfully loving lift.

Smiling, lovingly, as well, Derrick Junior intervenes, "All right, you two…."

Now, looking at him, "My Son," I tell Derrick Junior: "the Good, and my Wife," looking back at her, now; "is indeed one of the greatest things to ever happen to me. Equally, I love you, both, so very much!"

More, if you're to look close enough, you'll see, quite feasibly, a few diamond-shaped tears drop right from my happily tearful eyes. I even intend to buy *Xina*, or my wildly wonderful wife, a very nice-sized diamond ring once my ship sails right in. It'll be a little something to just show my absolute appreciation of her.... Plus, that very manly son of mine will be paid back his gloriously generous gift since given to me—without fail, or doubt: "Thanks, once again, Son, 'or, my Son—the Good!'" I cry out, absolutely, for absolute joy.

I just can't help hugging him, and lovingly, all over again. Do so right before we get right down, to business, and seriously. Produce! Or, producing productivity is some pretty serious business..., or production. Nor can I help thinking about one of life's biggest dichotomies: That, the good and the bad just love each other despite their hatred of one another. So similarly, I'm only too goddamn glad that the Bad hasn't visited me, so necessarily, or won't be visiting me...: OOOH-WEE—YIPPEE...!

Book II: The Bad

Fate
Waits
Upon
No
One

Prelude

Act I

Scene 1

Portsmouth, Virginia

On a wet, gray, and late—or, an un-welcoming morning or even day in late fall of 2001; at a small and villa-styled apartment of a home; on the outer edge of the military town; the telephone rings, and raucously, inside the dark, little, and cram-full, or chock-full bed-room.

DINNG!

DINNNG! "Damn!" I gnarl, and grimacing, and even turning over in my utterly uncomfortable bed. I just need a brand new mattress, desperately. DINNNG...! "...DAMIT...!" I snarl, again, and rising, up. I just snatch the telephone—up, from where it's lain right on top of the night stand next to my bumpy bed: "Hello!" I answer, and, angrily. Lately, I've been angered, and absolutely, right, by my lack of campaign funding. Where, too, am I going to get the necessary money for a new mattress?

"Good morning, Martin," speaks Bo Buford, or my current campaign manager.

"Morning, Bo. What's up 'or down?'" I ask, eagerly, if not anxiously.

"Well," says Bo, "Monday's your big day, in which you'll announce, officially, your candidacy for Mayor of our great city."

Now isn't the time to tail off or speak out of turn.... So, I choose my words carefully, and, very: "Yes, indeed, that'll be the big day. I'm trusting, as well, that it'll be smooth sailing, afterwards, and especially, financially—"

"But, of course—and, why wouldn't it? After all, you're a militarily up-standing retiree...; who so appreciates the political, social, and economic climate—among other things, right, here, in our military town. Particularly, you realize such atmosphere after the terrible terror attacks of September the eleventh...."

"Thanks, Bo, for the words of encouragement, or support. I so value it—yet, it's going to take a great deal more...." I comment, realistically, and roundly—restless. I'd expected to have far more reserve funds. DAMN...! I implode, or better, explode internally. Damn, that woman and child both...! Almost, certainly, they're crushing me, so circularly, right, with their damned financial demands. Focus. I try to do such, focus, while banging a super-tight and left fist right on my bouncy bed—WHAM! Or, BAM...!

"...I know that it's going to require far more than just words to truly topple your opponents. And, please, don't worry..., because you're without a doubt, a far superior candidate—or, man. Now, are there any sorts of loose ends, which you'd like tighten up, any, at all, before your big day?"

"No," I lie, out-rightly. I'm almost ashamed to tell anyone about their super shame-less games.... That my ex-wife and my ex-daughter both have been, un-fortunately, and utterly, un-loving, and un-supportive of me: or, my great big bid for a mayor-ship. Why can't they just understand...?

"Martin," Bo asks, "you're still there?"

I reply, reluctantly, if not half-heartedly, "Of course, and I'll talk with you, later. Also, have a good—or, a great weekend, Bo, because you're most deserving of such."

"Why thank you, Boss, and the same to you."

"Thanks, again, and good-bye."

"Bye-bye, for now," Bo Buford ends our truth or dare, conversation. He's done so—perhaps, unknowingly, and utterly.

Scene 2

Truthfully, I'm just anxious or worried or even threatened right by my ex-wife's, and especially, by my ex-daughter's dispute, if not vain-gloriously vile vendetta against me. I've to devise a much better plan, most definitely, to deal with the two: one of whom, I owe some back alimony to; the second of whom, I owe some back child-support to.

Up! I just need to be very prepared for any if not all attacks onto my campaign or my person—me. Now isn't the time to back away or sit back or even lie back, and restlessly, or apprehensively, in fear of whatever damnably dark threats are out there. Most likely, they're right out there, and family-like or not, waiting very impatiently to do me in, expertly. I'm now up and about straightening up or out my little bed of big bumps.

...If my little military retirement pay—or, if my little civilian job as a free-lance journalist—both, were much bigger—then, I'd afford a damn new mattress. Instead, I'm counting if not hoarding every damned dollar just like it's the very last one that I'll ever see or have. Why don't those two roundly revengeful females just let me be—free, financially, awhile, longer...?

That's correct or, so right. For, it takes lots of damn money to keep up and even win my politically tight fight; plus, to do so with all my goddamn might...! Though, today, I suppose that I'm all right. I'm alive and well—up, fighting, for damn sure, for my beautifully bright future. That's dressed, none the less, with some undeniably dim doubt.

"GODDAMNIT…!" I just squawk, seeing a hole in my house robe that's lying over the bouncy bed's railing. I'm just about to put it on. But, not before I just bang a super-tight and right fist on my very lumpy bed, angrily: WHANG! That's right; as, I'm angered, anxiously, all over again. Where are all of my political contributors? Huh?

…I'm now stepping right into my house shoes that're under my bed. "OUCH…!" I screech, hitting my left foot, so hard, against the bed's bottom railing. When are things going to happen just as planned, uh?

…Woefully unwonted worry wants to set in, as well as an absolutely atypical ache. My left foot is starting to hurt. Ouch! I'm again attempting to get about, moving round the little bumpy bed. I manage to put on that holey house robe of mine without hurting myself, yet again.

Worry, anger, and the like, all have a starkly dark way of just ruining one's morning, or damned day. Yet, I'm not about to let it just get me down; or, just take me down to a nakedly dark, hard, cold, and dirty, and even shaky ground: so grumbling, and blundering, or fumbling, away: No damn way…! I say again: NO DAMN WAY…!

After I put my house robe on…, I'll leave the room. But, not, before I halt right in front of the little looking glass, or the mirror, of the bedroom's dresser. Rightly, to see just how fantastic fret or fantastic fury is influencing my being, or me. No doubt, that I've my just or fair share of grey hairs and patchy wrinkles, already, at the not so tender age of 40—41; for, both ages are roundly relevant or intwined inextricably.

Likewise, it's nearly impossible to ever look good or even great if one hasn't certain things—and, quite, certainly, if such things aren't pending…: genuine peace, health, love, happiness, and success, (and even a little rest…); all of which, almost, always, necessitate or even demand a certain level of commitment, perseverance, and courage, that ought to lead to some honor….

Shouldn't one's life be right about super self-determination and all…? I just question the mirror, and believing that it's not about to lie or betray me, none, at all. For the most part, I've almost always had such things, courage, perseverance, and, commitment, and, even, success, and so forth. Yet, well, I'm not altogether sure that such things will be….

Honestly, I'm so goddamn tired of putting others before me, and, to what actual avail? Well, it's been to some avail seemingly. Since, life is just about to allow me some political power that should only increase. After such, others will then hustle and even bustle their butts or asses right for me, most, specifically. That's correct, as there'll be no more damn rippin' and runnin' in a semi-state of employment; grappling, if not groveling, quite grotesquely, for some free-lance and journalistic work, here, there, and every where—or, part-time. MOVE IT! Since life just goes on—but, not, necessarily, upwards. Or rather, *fate waits upon no one.*

Scene 3

Right, on the move, I've since left my little bedroom of a big bumpy sanctuary. I'm now moving right toward the kitchen. It's where I so plan to settle right on some serious support: A pretty poisonous stick of smoke, and, maybe, a poisonously dark drink; both of which, I probably shouldn't flavor or savor so very early. But, life has its damned problems, doesn't it? One of which, problem, is still my real lack of political funding. "I'll be damned!" I gripe, gravely, and grappling right with the notion of feasible failure....

Scene 3
Continued

Now, I'm entering the colorlessly small space of a kitchen.... Again, once, I get my due or political power..., I'll move on—up, in the world: pay bills, mainly, and—even more, up-grade my residence—or, living quarters. I could even use a brand new car, some brand new clothes, and so on. After all, I'll have a spanking brand new image to up-hold, without doubt or fail.

At present, I'm just opening the small icebox, which, it-self, has some huge holes in it: "Damnit...!" I snap, irritably. I'm sensing that I just may not have enough money, this month, to fill up the refrigerator with food. That's right! All of my damned bills are just killing me, figuratively, and literally.

More, what in the world could've or would've caused if not possessed me, to invest so much of my hard-earned or hard-won money; right, in the circularly cold, callous, or, cruel, and even, crumbly stock market...? Damn, those terrible terrorists of September the eleventh...! ...Anger and unwonted worry—both, have begun to set right in; or, both have moved right in, for the potently poisonous kill.

A part of my being—or, more, precisely, a part of my body has begun to ache and shake..., so implausibly. Not, to worry, though, as I'm just about to light up something sweet and even drink something sweeter; both of which should lessen my shakable state of being—or fate, and its darkly stark-naked ache.

I just reach right through one of those huge holes in the refrigerator; reaching, right, for a freshly refrigerative, or a freshly refrigeratory smoke, and chilly or cold yet cozy and constant but even so, a not so smooth bottle of Gin. It's some win-gin. Or, it's what I so like to call it, *win-gin*. Next, I make haste to indulge both poisons. Do so, right, after I shut the refrigerator's door.

That is, I'm now getting a very nice-sized glass from the dish-rack and then pouring myself a very nice-sized drink.

Then, I get a lighter from one of the cabinet's drawers.... In no time, at all, both will serve me—or, so serve my corporeal halves: the one cool— and, the other warm; both of which are almost always willing and ready to do battle against one another—or, with some other. That's right—or correct. As, my brain and my gut both—or my whole being, can't and won't continue to be shaken, aching. I just decide to head out-doors or out-side, where upon I'll do far more than just coddle both poisons, most cozily.

While heading toward the out-door patio, the door-bell rings, roundly, and, so loudly. "Damn…!" I gripe, quite, grumpily, and just assuming a quiet morning…. I turn around on my some-what worn-down heels to see who's at the door. Typically, I hear a person when she or he comes…, calling, for one reason or another reason. But, with my pre-occupation…, and all, I've been a bit bothered…: mentally, emotionally, and, physically, and, even, spiritually. Focus!

…Peeping right through the front door's little peep-hole, I've to now focus right on the fairly tall, lightly tan, and surely slim, yet totally toneful, or strawberry blonde; that's just about to ring my door bell, again. Yet, she's so interrupted as I open the door up, almost, immediately. The super shrill sound of some damned door-bell's ding-dong is something that I can do without— no doubt. There's absolutely no need to bring on some sound-bound—head-ache—or, some utterly unpropitious pang, pain.

"Mornin' Love…," speaks Sira Simpson, or my very current business associate, confidante, friend, girl friend, and all.

She's dressed or well-fitted, and, smartly, in an un-colorfully crisp yet sensibly stylish slack set…; whose blackish-gray shirt adds even more style to Sira's gray suit. "Mornin'," I just reciprocate and am surprised, somewhat, to see her so un-announced…; "Do we've a date…?"—I ask but am cut right off.

Sira cuts right in, "No, not really." In a pair of black-heeled shoes, she then steps right through the front door of my little place. Or, she just invades my little space with a big brown bag right in tow. Her purse and all is in it— big brown bag, more than likely. "…I'm just surprising you with a nice-sized breakfast, and all. Besides, we've to talk…, before I go to work," Sira adds, in an utterly and un-characteristically low voice.

"Oh?" I remark, shutting the front door.

Scene 4

Indoors, she puts down that big brown bag on the kitchen's counter; which has some sort of really big breakfast in it, bag, most, probably. Next, Sira takes her black purse from the bag and then the rest of the food stuff.... "What do you've for me or us...?" I ask, curiously, and moving toward her.

Now she's taking every single thing right out of that very big brown bag...: darkly caffeinated coffee; golden hash browns; thick ham and cheese omelets; toasty English muffins; and, tasty-looking fruit-salad. "Hmmm...," I murmur, "everything smells and looks good," and requiring no real answer to my question....

"Before we eat, Love, I've to just tell you—"

"What?" I interject, impatiently.

"Well," states Sira, slowly, "you may just want to light up..., or drink down..., or even do both—"

"What is it, Woman?"

She starts saying, again, "Well, I've since spoken right with a distant colleague or a journalistic friend of mine—"

"Oh?" I question, nosily, if not restlessly.

"There's just no easy way to say it—"

"Say what?" I interpose—or, question, yet again, and curiously, if not anxiously, or even demandingly with more than just a damn demanding tone.

"There are some roundly ruinous rumors that've been just circulating, and, quite, circularly, about your financial situation, or rather, your financial predicament."

"Oh?"

"Yes. It just seems that my friend has since spoken with someone or another that's accusing you of being a damnably dark dead-beat."

"What?" I ask, once again, lighting it right up: my poisonous stick of smoke.... It and my poisonous drink both have waited—only, too, goddamn, patiently, for me.... Also, there's a super sheer scowl right on Sira's lightly tan-colored face now; whose roundly blackish-brown brows are raised now; whose starkly dark-blue-colored eyes are pieced now—(and, right, on me...); whose slenderly small nose is squinted, now; plus, whose lusciously labored lips are drawn in now—but, not, for long.

"Listen..., Love, I've since sensed or even suspected that you've had some financial difficulties. After all, you've since insinuated such. Still, well, the thought—just, has never occurred to me—"

I just come right out with the dreadfully stark-naked truth: "That I'm behind on my damn alimony and damn child-support, payments?"

"Well, yes."

"Who's spreading, and, so regrettably, the goddamned—regrettable—yet, real rumors…?" I inquire, puffing, so poisonously, and un-easily, or even agitatedly.

"I just can't divulge such source, rightly. For there's this thing called journalistic ethics, or integrity, which must be considered and all."

I just flavor a much-extended swallow of my Gin, or poison. Then, I demand out-rightly and not that politely: "Ascertain or determine who's out to get me…. 'Or, take me down to a circularly cold, or cruel, or even callous ground of an under-world….'" Though, we ought to suspect those roundly rotten if not roundly revengeful and boastfully bombastic bitches or bastards: *Mizani* Montgomery, plus Maxine Montgomery. Why haven't they found a way to just drop their last names—(or, my last name)—right, from their first names? Huh? Worry now wants to re-visit me in a darkly sad or a darkly bad way.

"Hey," Sira just tells me, and, seemingly, so sympathetically; "Martin Montgomery, you can share your problems right with me. Plus, I'm almost, always, so willing and ready. To, help you out of some utterly un-joyous jam, beginning right with this piece of advice. You've to just pay your damn bills at any and all costs, or without doubt—fail. No would-be politician should or would ever let his or her personal finances be an issue—"

"Woman, PLEASE…!" I just snap, coldly, and am chilled, circularly, right, by Sira's seemingly un-sympathetic sentiment, or damned see-sawing: zig-zagging, and wig-wagging. Doesn't she know—just, how god-damn hard times are for me: mentally, emotionally, physically, spiritually, economically, and socially, and even politically, and so forth? On the surface, all that's been good has since gone right away: full-employment, full-credit, full-clout, full-contributions, and the like.

"…Don't bark at me, MISTER, for I'm only trying to help or advise you…!"

Our eyes lock, as one, and intensely; our breaths are shallow, or one-dimensional; we both just want to step back from each other; or just turn our eyes away from one another, on the face of it.

Sira then squawks, with a definite demand of her own: "WELL, SAY SOMETHING…!"

"Now isn't the time to inflame 'or hassle' me…, WOMAN!" I answer up, and anxiously, and even gloweringly. Worry, anger, and dread, and even Sira herself are all visiting me in a badly dark or a badly sad way.

"Please, Martin, don't just put me off—IF SO, you may just regret it," proclaims Sira, backing up, some.

"You're now threatening me…, MISSY?" I question, glaringly, and, most guardedly…. Because, one can never be too goddamn safe…. Plus, my next response reflects such: "Pretty please, just leave my home and just leave me alone, NOW!"

She steps back even more than before. "FINE…!" Sira whines, a wee bit and then far more: "And, what about breakfast—to hell with it…! I'll just take mine back with me…," re-packing that big brown bag; "Also, when you settle down…, some, or perhaps, a great deal—then, call me…. But, not, one goddamn minute…! As I leave, I just can't help wondering—"

"What now, WOMAN?"

"Why've you put your-self out there as some kind of up-standing man that's suitable for public office? I've never known some damn dead-beat of a politician. So please, MARTIN, hurry up and pay your damned bills—"

"You arrogant, condescending, manipulative, and power-hungry, and even so-called political pundit…, 'or political junkie of a BITCH, or even journalistic whore—'"

"WHACK…!" Sira just slaps my face with all her damn might; "How dare you patronize or analyze or even criticize and ostracize me, for meeting important people, or doing important things, and going important places—"

"SLAP…!" I now whack Sira's face with all my damn might. "GET OUT…!" I just demand, and am now done digressing or regressing, goddamn dilly-dallying.

Now, she's so speechless, and preparing to leave or get out…. That's correct—or, right. Grabbing that big brown bag, Sira scuffles un-steadily, yet steadily, enough—on; right, out the front door of my little safe haven of a home, or house. But, not, before she adds more abuse to the damage…: "Play the game right, MARTIN, and be very good or better at it. Or, you'll just end up losing, for damn sure!"

Scene 4
Continued

With fantastic force, the front door shuts right behind her—SLAM!

Finishing my poisonous smoke but not my poisonous drink…, I just gulp down the last of my *win-gin*. Next, I drop my cigarette's butt in the wet glass. Then, I just hurl the damn glass at the goddamn front door, or the very last thing—that, that journalistic Jezebel has touched of mine. SMASH! I'm no damn clown that's bound to be wound way—up, or put way—down, by the goddamned likes of Sira Simpson. CRACK…! And, the shattering of the broken glass is sounding out, and soundly, or roundly, in my head. CRACK! CRACK! CRACK!

Shuffling on my heels, I need some fresh air and a fresh start. That is, once again, I'm headed outdoors. But, not, before I get some more poison; which will accompany me, rather, comfortably, outside; where upon I aim, so absolutely, to continue devising a pretty precise plan; which will see me right through the blackishly fiery fire. It's a fantastically if not a fierily black fire. That so wants to burn all of my deliciously good dreams—up. Such just can't and won't go up in flames or fire: my definite desires and my dire needs—or, delicious dreams. Also, I'll eat my big breakfast, later. Because, I'm not one to just discard or reject free food. Is there anything that's free of charge, ever, honestly? Focus, now. Or, no damn wig-wagging, zig-zagging!

Act II

Scene 1

...What an utterly un-lovely or a damnably dark sight out here on this little deck of a patio. After having fallen way behind with my big bills and all, I've since down-graded my living arrangements. Damn, Fool! How could I've been such a goddamn blithering idiot, too; to allow my-self to be eaten alive—right, by damned loan sharks...? Goddamn them and those thoroughly terrible terrorists of September the eleventh! Needless, to say, that I'm firing one poison up, and even drinking the other poison down.... I feel, as well, as both poisons ease the utterly un-propitious pain or pang; so, un-rightly, that just loves to visit me or stay with me, un-propitiously, or, in-opportunely.

I'm even sitting at one small set of two very small sets of patio tables, here, on the small patio of a small shelter. But, just, how safe am I, really, from the nakedly dark forces that're just out there in the dark-naked distance? That so-called journalist of a woman—or, Sira Simpson, wants to re-visit me, even, if surrealistically, or, most unbelievably. I take another super stretched swallow of my poisonous drink.... I'm even watching the super sweet smoke from my other poison just cloud such super sour scene, or vision. I just want to stretch out or relax.... Yet, I'm utterly un-able to do so. It's because of the smallness of this so-called place or very small space of a sanctuary.

DAMNIT! I screech and am very saddened, if not maddened right by the circularly cheerless circumstances of my fate.... It's just draped with utter un-certainty. I'm certain, though, that the woman who's now coming toward me with a very big claw hammer in her left hand is up to no goddamn good. That's right—or, correct! She's since clawed her way right back into my little life. Quite, possibly, Sira may even have a super sharp knife.... And, to think

57

that I'd consider, ever, just asking her to be my wife—NEVER! Sira stops, suddenly, stepping back on the very narrow walkway. It leads up to and away from the back patio's screen door.

There, right, in the midst of some super sorry-looking landscape—or, wretchedly weathered trees, bushes, grass, and even flowers—some shouting sounds out: "I'll just let somebody else continue hammering some super solid sense right into that super hard head of yours…!"

Now, she's strutting away…; her head up in the roundly restricted air; and, her shoulders up-right; and, her steps super steady; and even, her bearing boastfully bombastic or, up-tight. "You over-bearing bitch of a bastard…!" I so bawl, being brought right back to actuality. It's the reality of my very real life. That's ruining, and roundly, my perspective of life—if not, my prospects for it—life, or the future: the good.

I growl, GODDAMN her! Then, I just watch that fantastically fallible female. She's disappearing right into a damnably dark morning even though it's very near ten o'clock. Sira is doing so, just, fading away, right, with some type of wickedly weird cape on, now. It's just flapping round about. It most definitely conceals the deadly weapon or even weapons that she's since taken to, quite senselessly. BOO, HOO…!

How sad—I think to myself—that things have since come to this: My prospectively planning or plotting to be rid of her, roundly, and even be rid of the roundly rotten forces…; which are posed so purposely to do me in, and, rather forcefully. I don't want to feel it, such force, none, at all.

Thus, I just flavor some more of both poisons…: the first of which, whose sweet smoke is just dying out in a little ceramic ashtray; the second of which, whose colorless liquid is just about gone; both of which, again, ought to just continue helping me get rid of, or just forget all about the starkly black demons. They're visiting me, most inconveniently: *Mizani* and Maxine.

After having savored, or rather, having so finished both poisons, my head is now much clearer; my heart is now much lighter; my body is now at ease; my spirit is just about to soar. For, I now want or need to go somewhere else. It's a place and a time where all is just fine—light, or bright, and right. That's so right…! Life and its little conquerable inhabitants—all, are mine to conquer…, still: just, like a colorful conqueror. That's conquering, colorfully, and, so circularly, some un-colorful yet candied and coy or crisp or even cold conquest of a female.

Scene 2
Subic Bay, Philippines
U.S. Naval Base Subic Bay—The Past

On an arid and clear yet dim or dark—or even sultrily late, but an interesting night in the late summer of 1980; in a seemingly small space of a discotheque near the U.S. Naval Base *Subic Bay*; a group of roundly raucous sailors have all gathered.

The aged, and small-sized, and even self-made man of a *Filipino* boss is standing high, if not standing out, right, at the front door of his large office. Such stand-point, almost, always, permits Papa-Boss both covert and overt opportunities; to just observe, so intermittently, the often disorderly comings and goings of his military clientele as well as his female employees; who're, un-incidentally, young, pretty, and shapely—female *Filipinos*.

Right, from my view-point, at a some-what sheltered table for two, I've a doggone good view, too, of the real goings-on. What's really going on, mostly, is that off-duty sailors just like me are all just trying to blow off some steam. It's an end-less stream of very steamy pressure, that's put upon us by our presser of an uncle—Uncle Sam: pressing productivity—or production—and, most un-propitiously.

So, we're all right here at Klub Kiwi, steaming, if not producing, or just pressing away. I can see plainly, also, a bunch of roundly raucous sailors, who're sitting at a particular table.... In my strong opinion, they're releasing just enough doggoned steam or steamy pressure: drinking enough; smoking enough; yakking enough; butt-watching enough, and so on.

I can see, even, that the boss-man—or, Papa-Boss is about done just standing by..., so idle, or stock-still. Quite, probably, those raucous sailors of drunkenly sexual leeches are just too doggone lovey-dovey for him, (or are they...); It's Papa-Boss, whose very well-known job is to take good care of the female employees that're in his employ. Once again, that man of a boss is about done just standing by; just, watching those lecherous leeches leech off of the female *Filipinos*, or employees, or even waitresses, and the like; whose appearances, manners, and so forth, are rather welcoming..., to say the very least.

What's more, most of the females are so touchy-feely or feely-touchy, enough, with the so colorfully dark clientele—or, leeches. They're all rowdy, and, roundly, if you're to ask me...; more, it's just as well. There's plenty of cozy conversing, butt-touching, and all, right, in between drinking, smoking, and the like. In particular, one *Filipino* female of a server or waitress is just seizing my utterly un-divided attention. And, I even plan to have her serve me. Do so, as soon as she's through serving that gang of raucous sailors their thickly dark poison. It's some darkly thick-looking beer, maybe.

I've to just greet or meet her.... I'm trusting, as well, that I'm looking all right..., especially, after having worked my butt or my ass off—all damn day. Uncle Sam even wanted me to stay, at work. Or, to put in some over-time, work, just, like there's no damned tomorrow: No goddamn way...! I'd to just say way under my breath..., of course. Aloud, I'd said, instead, that I switched duty right with somebody, supposedly. Yet, that someone ended up standing his own damned duty. Yippee!

Then, I just yipped and yipped right on: yipping, hopping, and, not, at all stopping until I ended up right here, at Klub Kiwi, on a fantastic Friday, night. That's so right—or, so correct.... It's even where I intend to satisfy my personal life. For, I'm in real need of a damn good wife: Somebody that's not going to give me any strife, ever. Or, stab or jab me in the back or the heart with a jaggedly sharp and big butcher's knife. That's right...! There'll be no sort of nastily tight fight, in which my wife takes some big bites right out of my manly might.

Now, he's right in my sight..., that man of a Papa-Boss; who's now joining those roundly raucous soldiers, and uninterestingly, yet grinningly, at their messy table. We know his name, already, but what's the boss-man's real game? Huh? Since, he's not about to tame anybody: no rasping sailor, or, no wiggly waitress, or, no one—at all. I just signal for that one female server—young, pretty, and shapely, raising my arm or my hand up, high. She'll serve me, for sure. Though, not, before Papa-Boss just has his way, whatever way that just happens to be. Or, I'll soon see without doubt or fail.

Scene 3

Most definitely, his style of dressing symbolizes Papa-Boss's success. Dressed in a super silvery slack set..., that boss-man is just sauntering on—over, to that table.... He's doing such, stepping, steadily, and right pass the rectangular-shaped dance floor; where upon dancers are dancing, dancingly, and, quite; whose dance floor is absolutely accommodative, accommodating a colorfully young disk-jockey or D.J...; whose playing of records—"Night Fever," and "Bad Girls," and all, has just about everyone up, dancing, away.

Approaching that table of raucous sailors..., the boss-man approaches them, rather, cordially: "Ho! Ho! Ho! And, how's it goin'..., Fellows?" asks

Papa-Boss, so grinningly. Continuing, on; "Y'all just out for a good time—as usual, uh? I'm sure that my girls are treatin' y'all all right—"

"They sure are...," answers an Oriental-looking male of a sailor.

Papa-Boss exclaims..., "Great! For I've the very best servers around town, servin'. Also, Fellows, know this—y'all releasin' some steam is almost always welcome—here."

"Thanks Papa-Boss...," says an African-looking sailor, male, "as our partyin' and all isn't always so easy to swallow.... But, you and the girls, or waitresses and all are totally tolerant of us. And, we all thank you for that!"

A pale-looking male or sailor speaks..., excitedly, "for damn sure...!" And, needless to say, that, that one female server in particular is just exciting him...: "Hey Babe—Mama! Please bring Daddy some more poison—or beer, you hear...?"

Bustling or hustling about..., the waitress acknowledges such request or crude or even lewd demand by waving, vivaciously. Nor would she dare to just wave off the pale-looking sailor.... Not, while the boss-man is still very much engaged in the comings and goings of things, people, and all, so round about. That's right; Papa-Boss will make some other rounds...; visit others' tables...; chit-chat with his circularly colorful or dark clientele, and so on.

The other two, or tan-colored males that're sitting at that messy table of raucous sailors are just drinking, smoking, and butt-watching, away.

"Well, Fellows," Papa-Boss states, "I've only wanted to wish y'all a good evenin' or a good night. Now, if there's anything—at all, that y'all want or need, further, to continue makin' it a good or a great night—then, please, don't hesitate—"

"We won't...," interjects one of the very tan-colored sailors...; whose interjection is being interrupted by a waitress that's colorfully if not scantily clothed...; who starts straightening right up the sailors' mess or messy table: cleaning the table; straightening chairs; emptying ash-trays, and the like.

Seemingly, the sailor is un-dressing her even more, sensually, if not, sexually, with his overly overt staring—or, bold body watching. All is taking place to the soulfully sexy sounds of Donna Summer's "I Feel Love."

"Don't worry..., Papa-Boss. Since all's well"—the Asian or Oriental-looking male just assures their greeter, or host, or even overly overt enabler; who's just about finished..., on the face of it, of enabling his roundly raucous regulars.

That, Papa-Boss doesn't mind, at all, if such sailors are just too damn feely-touchy or lovey-dovey or even touchy-feely with the female employees in his employ: "Y'all go right 'head and enjoy yourselves..., fully," the boss-man even interpolates, winking, superficially. He even adds, casually, if not naughtily: "Or, carry on, Sailors." Next, Papa-Boss saunters or moseys away. He's doing such just as casually as him having first moseyed or sauntered on, over, to the raucous sailors' table.

It's now high time for me to get right into the action, too. Or, descend right into some starkly dark-naked hell of a heaven. That's correct. Since, I'm just about to make my own damn move; or, move right in for the super-sweet kill, so figuratively. Again, I'm just signaling for that one female server..., in particular—young, pretty, and, shapely. I'm even raising my hand or arm—up. She'll soon serve me, for sure. Yippee!

Scene 4

I'm now firing it right up—poison. Yet, I only flavor or savor a puff or two before I kill it—or, before it kills me: my poisonously sweet smoke. I can't and won't allow any sort of smoke to cloud my vision of the future: or, my fantastically fabulous fate. It's so dressed with a super successful career, marriage—a wife, and even children—very long-lasting love, and all.

And, all I've to do is just put my very best face or just put my very best foot—forward. Do so, especially, if I intend to get with that one female of a server..., so, in particular: young, pretty, and shapely—*Filipino* waitress. She's now coming right toward me, smilingly, or seductively, and fatefully. YIPPEE! Who's really going to seduce who...? Huh?

With a super or a submissively sweet smile of her own, she greets me, smiling, and, most smilingly—now: "Hi there—"

"Hi," I answer back, quickly.

"What'll it be...?" asks the young, pretty, and very shapely waitress, seductively, or quite seemingly.

Right, before I give her a welcomingly wide smile of my own, if not a seductively sweet smile of my own, I respond: "I'll have something heavy or un-even or even dry—"

"What about some house-beer—"

"What's that?" I question, a bit embarrassingly if not ignorantly.

"It's the usual house-special, or some beer that's brewed..., locally."

"All right," I consent..., curiously, and am curious, still, about such beer...; "I'll just have to trust your suggestion..., and all. By the way, please forgive those roundly raucous sailors if they're too damn rowdy—"

"Thanks.... But, I'm rather used to it, or, their rowdiness..., and all. Besides, I, almost, always, pride myself on hangin' right with the very best of them—"

"Oh?"

"…Why sure…, because they're only releasin' some steam…, and the steamier, the better…. Since, such, almost, certainly, means more work and more money for me…."

I'm not exactly taken aback—or surprised, at all, and commenting, so colorfully: "Well, then, why don't we just try releasing 'or makin'' our own 'damn' steam, on a little 'or a big' date?" I ask, eagerly.

"You're askin' me out—"

"Of course…. And, why not…?" I say—then, cross-question, smiling, so smilingly, or seductively. Once more, who'll seduce who…? Huh?

"A proper date—"

"Of course…. And, 'pretty' please, may I've the privilege or honor of knowing your name—"

"Oh!" The fantastically fine female exclaims; "Sorry! I'm *Mizani* and you're—"

"I'm Martin and am at your service…."

"…I think not, just, yet…," speaks *Mizani* with a sweetly, if not, a singularly seductive smile; "since, I'm most at your service, obviously. Now, I'd better get that drink before you forget all about it."

"That's not going to happen, '*Luv*.'"

"It sure isn't since I'm just about to get it for you…. So, you just sit right, still, and I'll be right back…. By the way, Papa-Boss will be very glad that you've chosen his house-special. It's not cheap and all."

"Huh-uh," I just mutter or mumble or even grumble—shudder. Since, I'm not at all about spending lots of money on my drinking pleasure, tonight. I've bills that ought to come first…, for darn sure. Still, I truly like *Mizani's* get-up-and-go—or, energy. Up close, or, in person, she's really energetic or, so full of life—lively: I can just tell that she has some spring in her step or steps. But, what does it all mean in actuality or in reality?

Could we ever have a real or a true life, together? Or, would she even consider being my wife: the great love of my life; who'll never give me any type of damn strife…? Or, better, would she mind living a life that's dictated, most, doggedly, by Uncle Sam and the very doggoned likes of him? They're damnably dark dictators that just like to dictate others' lives. Do such, while even toting their jaggedly big butchers' knives…. Still, I'd like for our spirits to be entwined—*Mizani's* and mine.

Scene 4
Continued

Mizani yelps, or snaps her fingers, snappily, "Hey! Don't go driftin' off on me or anything like that."

"I won't 'or can't…,' to be sure…, '*Luv*,'" I state, so single-heartedly, being brought right back to reality. Is this real, my getting with her, *Mizani*?

"…It's just about time that the party here starts turning to, truly, or being very busy. So, just sit back—and, loosen up—or, let go. Because your drink's comin' right up," *Mizani* tells me, turning to—or around.

That is, she turns on her heels…. But, not, before her brownish-black-colored eyes, and my blackish-brown-colored eyes so lock, together; or, not, before I'm so merely mesmerized by her nakedly dark loveliness or, head of hair; whose shinily mid-night-black color is shining, away; like the blackish-white-colored light that's right above my table; whose whitish-black-colored light is just lighting up her lovely face…; whose naturally shaped brows are centered, circularly, right, over those slant-like and brownish-black-colored eyes, and even toweringly thick lashes of hers; whose dark thickness doesn't over-shadow her pointedly short nose that's since twitched, so cutely; whose cute twitching can't cover up; or, divert any attention from the super sheer silkiness of her very pretty pecan-colored skin that's glowing, away; like the mid-night stars that're stalking the starkly blackish-gray or starkly grayish-black-colored sky of a night.

Is *Mizani* purely pretty poetry in motion, motioning for me to kiss her gorgeously glittery lips? They're lustrously luscious lips glittering away. Or, dazzling, like the colorfully multi-colored lights that're just lighting the disco right up. No…, I decide, for now. Since, there'll be plenty time to kiss—or rather, to risk my stark-naked or super stark singleness.

I'm once more just about to fire it right up—poison. I do so, too, and, successfully. Next, I just sit back—or, just relax, and then let the poisonously sweet smoke just move me, quite relaxingly. Yet again, it can't and won't be allowed to cloud my very vivacious vision of the future: It's so garbed, very vivaciously, with all that's light, pretty, right, and good. Neither will I permit anything dark, ugly, wrong, or bad to happen to me, her, or even us. If the truth were told, things are starting to spin, spinning all around in a circularly closed circle; or, inside of my head; or, inside of my very single-track mind. Is time on my side…?

…I probably shouldn't have had the few yet stiff shots of Gin or *win-gin*, right, at the barracks prior to my having come here, at Klub Kiwi. Still, I intend to put a brand spanking new spin on my singleness…. Light it right up with *Mizani*, and singly. She's since disappeared only to re-appear, smilingly, if not seductively, in the naked smokiness of my super sweet seduction. Per, chance, it'll be a time and a place that's so in-tolerable or, so in-supportable to some double-standard. This is to say, that, I'll almost always set the single-standard or standards for her to just follow, without doubt or—fail. And, with some luck, the Lord will help her if she should ever fail....

Act III

Scene 1

The Present

I'm now hearing the sounds of sirens. They're either the sirens of an ambulance, or the sirens of a police cruiser..., cruising by. Then, I just think, so suddenly, and sourly, of that super sour siren of a woman—my ex-wife—*Mizani*. That's very correct. She's no longer some sweetly seductive, young, and lovely, and even shapely server serving me.

But, instead, *Mizani* is dogging me, most doggedly, with that doggone daughter of hers, Maxine, or Maxi. They're making, so constantly, doggoned dark demands upon my person or poor me. Yet, I can't and won't be poor for much longer. Just as soon as my ship sails into port, there'll be some serious changes—or, up-grades, to my life, or status, and stature.

...I'd so tried to raise *Mizani*—up. Yet, she just kept right on taking or pushing us—both—down: right, to the damn ground just like damned earth-worms. Sure, I'd a militarily journalistic career; plus, an exotic wedding; and, a so-called—lovely marriage; and, even, an un-submissive wife; plus, an un-submissive child; the fourth of whom, wanted only to use me as a super solid step-ladder to a far better life; and, the fifth of whom, wanted only to follow, and solidly, in her mother's fantastically faulty foot-steps: stepping, right, on all that I've ever held dear. It was never an enduring relationship with either. Neither do I miss it...: The past that's been padded or clad, so circularly, and colorfully, and even, callously, right, with colorful calamity. Goddamn them females...! I just explode, heatedly. They're quite simply—bad news...! I'm imploding..., needlessly: DOGGONIT!

And, I just need to calm right down. Or, strategize. Actually, I needn't continue strategizing; or, just, planning a plan, to pay the females—back; or, planning a plan, to pay the females—off. I've decided, since, to just give the two officially written *IOU's* in lieu of some verbal *IOU's*.... Such ought to soothe over or smooth out their darkly doggone demands.... Those damned financial parasites...!

Once again, *Mizani* and Maxi both are very vicious vultures, vying to devour me, financially, and unmercifully. Why couldn't I've had the courage to just poison them—both? Instead, I've been left with my own god-damn poison poisoning me; …thoroughly, I'm not altogether sure of, just, yet.

Needless to say, that it's now calling out my name, and, so loudly: my poison. It's even waiting for me rather patiently—but, not, for much longer. Since, I'm just about to leave this little tiny space of a safe haven, or back patio. Also, I can hear, smell, see, and, touch, and even, taste, already, the poisonously sweet smoke as it moves in for the kill. I'll let, too, some sweetly poisonous *win-gin* accompany such smoke as it moves…. Now, I'm moving or getting right up from where I've sat in a semi-state of nothingness. What's more, nothing is going to stand in the way of my prospective prosperity—or, success, NOTHING! As I best be very well dressed for all that moves toward killing my political career, or me.

Scene 2
Later That Afternoon

DINNG…! "Goddamn…!" I just squawk, being awaken, most in-appropriately: DINNNG…! "I'll be goddamned!" I scowl, gloweringly. My scowling and glowering aren't nearly enough, though, to stop the telephone from sounding or howling out. So, I just make haste, unsteadily, to answer it. But, not, before my lumpy bed so hampers my ability or capacity to turn over or get up. Having gotten up…, I'm just snatching the damn phone...: "Hello!" I answer and not at all nicely or politely.

"Hello Martin," speaks the femininely soft voice.

Oh! No! I'm where…? Or, better yet, I've been where, day-dreaming, apparently, about her. The female that's right on the telephone…. She's been in my day-dream and is now very much in my life…. OH, NO…! What sort of strife is accompanying her dangerously dark and jagged knife…?

…I need some light, and turning on the little lamp that's atop the little night-table. She could even be in my sight. That's right; will the female come to bite me; or, have some kind of fight with all of her damn might, tonight? I really need some height, or have a super tight fist: be very well prepared for whatever the damned female doles out.

"Martin," speaks the femininely soft voice, again. In fact, the voice is so low as to be almost in-audible…. Is the female on the low-down or down-low and just won't let go…? Huh—heave-ho…!

"Yes, and hello *Mizani*," I answer up, a wee-bit more, politely, or, nicely. For she's real: or, the god-damned invader of my once dark and now light day-dream of a nakedly nasty nightmare...; "I haven't heard from you in some time—"

"Yes, I know.... I'd planned to call you way before—now. But, I've been roundly reluctant to do so because of our last encounter," states *Mizani* in her way down to the ground—voice.

"Yeah...!" I say and am now sitting up right. I'm even up-tight, some, still; "I'm a little sorry about that. But, you just pushed too damn hard—"

"I was only after my money..., Martin. It's lots of money that's very much wanted and needed for me and Maxi—both, to go on livin'—"

"Please, *Mizani*, don't start—"

"WHAT? I'm still after my—our damn money..., MARTIN! We're livin' hand-to-mouth in goddamn hand-me-downs and all. Frankly, I'm about finished...! Bein' down like some god-damned down-and-out clown," *Mizani* informs me, in an utterly un-feminine voice of anger, or rage..., clearly. Plus, I've known the entire time—that, that soft-spoken voice of hers has been only make-believe, or made-up..., quite, dreadfully; "Once, again, I'm done bein' down...! Do you hear me, MARTIN?"

"Woman, PLEASE—just settle down!" I squall, and shivering, some.

My words ricochet, so roundly, and raucously, if not loudly, from her big fat mouth: "SETTLE DOWN? You're kiddin'—or, crazy! To ever think that I'm not about ready, to saddle right up, or saddle right down—for, the damned fight of my life! And, I'll fight you, MARTIN, with all of my damn might! That's right! I'll even fight you, TONIGHT...!"

"There's really no need to get all up-tight! Take some nastily big bites right out of me, 'or pitiable or poor me...!'" Now, deep dark dread is visiting me rather unwelcomingly.

"WHY NOT...?" *Mizani* asks, quickly, in a tone of voice that's since risen, even, more.

I answer up—or back even quicker, "Because, I've since decided that I'll just give you and Maxi both officially written *IOU's*—"

She interjects—or, objects..., demandingly: "STOP IT! We've gone—already, through enough changes—or arbitrators, lawyers, the law, the court, and all—but, NO GODDAMN MORE, MARTIN! It's now high time for you to—JUST, pay up, or else—"

"WHAT?" I probe, and, some-what, painfully. I'm even standing up, in pain, some. Since, this female of a fantastic foe has begun to pain me or go against my aim, or, aims. I also aim to get rid of her. It's for the best—right, now; but, not, before I question her amid my feeling some utterly un-pretty pang: "Do you intend to just keep spreading our nasty laundry round about?

Or, just, vilifying me right in the eyes of folks that matter, 'to me personally and professionally?' HUH?"

Some long-drawn-out silence ensues until I myself slice right through it with my own damn knife: "SPEAK UP! Woman…!" I demand, doggedly. For, I'm not about to be dogged or just continue being dogged right by the doggone likes of *Mizani* Montgomery; or, some miserably fed-up and utterly un-feminine female—or even fantastically fallible and far-out—*femme fatale*.

"I'm so finished talkin'—as a matter of fact, I'm goin' to just let my devotedly dutiful daughter do the rest of the goddamned talkin'. So, just, stay tuned…, MISTER!" *Mizani* ends our back and forth or utterly un-civilized conversation—BAM! It's the super shrill sound of her having slammed, most spitefully, the telephone right down, on me, or, on us; or even our real need to resolve, roundly, the issue or issues that're plaguing us, or *Mizani*, Maxi, and me. Right, now, I see, too, that I'd better be very well prepared for some overly onerous onslaught onto my person or poor or even pitiable me. Focus.

Hours earlier, didn't I say it: That, I best be very well dressed for all that moves toward killing me, or my political career? Some poison will do it. Or, it'll kill what's plaguing me, if only, too, temporarily. It's none other than those monstrously malicious females…. Already, I can taste the two poisons: the one smoky, and the other smokier, so to speak. I still intend to win, of course, with the help of some stark-naked *win-gin*. After I flavor or savor my pretty patient if not potent poisons, I'll plot another plan of action, possibly, and, quite. Focus, now!

I'm now moving in for the kill or, to be killed, figuratively. Literally, I'm just making my way to the little kitchen…. There, I won't stay long. Or, it won't take that long for me to turn—to. Though, the darkly early night is crashing down and right on me—hard, and really. Yet, the very big bumps in my bumpy bed, fortunately, will help pad the starkly dark crash.

Scene 3

I've myself since crashed or landed, rather unsteadily, onto my lumpy or bumpy bed of a pad or, padding. Also, why couldn't it be some other day than—or, besides, Thursday? Monday will be here, soon, enough. At which time, I'll be moving ahead…, most, certainly. Veering my position right on the little barbaric bunk of a bed, I try to get more comfortable. I even loosen up the belt of my holey bed-robe. They're holes that the two females—or, the two foes, want to shoot right at, or chop right through.

I'm about through, too, being nice to the two. One of whom, I just can't help thinking all about. But, not before I veer my position, again. I hope not to just toss and turn…: see-saw—or, zig-zag—or, even, wig-wag, around.

What's more comfortable, having one's legs all stretched out or some other way...? While lying back or down, I'm opening up and then closing my tired eyes. They've seen lots of unwanted things, or people, lately. Nor do I've to tell you—that, as of late, I've been set back, monetarily. It's fine, for now, since all that'll change. Hooray...! In three days, or this coming Sunday, my biggest mayoral fund-raiser will be held..., however, un-officially, yet un-reservedly. What does a day or so matter..., anyway, or anyhow, uh?

That aside..., I'll secure some more work as a free-lance journalist, to help pay my bills—right, off, of course. Otherwise, I just stand to be killed, so figuratively. Why haven't my pretty potent poisons accompany me right to bed? Their sound, sight, smell, and feel, and even taste are welcomed, quite definitely. Since, the sound of that super sour siren screaming at me, sourly, if not scoffing at me, isn't enough, already. I'm hearing her and seeing her..., all over, again. DAMN...! Why can't and won't she just leave me, and my thoughts, alone, huh? Opening my eyes, rather, quickly, I ought not to drift back to such time and such place: when, the two of us crossed an ugly, if not an utterly ultra-fine line.

Tossing and turning, on this little bed of a lumpy or a bumpy bunk of mine—that, time and place is gnawing right at my mind: DAMNIT...! Focus now—or, relax—or, even, rest...! I'll need to be rested if not very well rested for the fight that's imminent, un-doubtedly: or, in, if not, on the cards—Tarot Cards, that is. *Mizani* is coming right toward me, right, on the face of it...: GODDAMNIT...! Hers has a fantastically ferocious frown on it, face. Still, I won't dare back away or back down. But, instead, I'll just face her right back down, to the nakedly and the damnably dark, hard, cold, dirty, and shaky, and even dangerous, or deathly ground.

I ought not to feel like such a little silly clown, either, for being taken in—right, by the damned likes of *Mizani*: just, like Sira, or even some other seductively un-submissive female. They all ought to submit..., smilingly, un-saltily, or lovingly, and, most supportingly; right, to a man that wants to lift them up, quite accordingly, right, to his philosophy of life; and, right, to his methodology, by which it ought to be so lived—their lives. Just, let the man wear his pretty, paternal pants, almost, always...! I'm now throwing the little light blanket over me.... Given that, I'm shaking and even aching..., a little. Steady, or settle down—FOCUS!

...I'm now focusing right on that female—or, would-be woman; and, how, exactly, I'll pay her back vice an *I.O.U.*—cash: how else...? I'll cash in my own brand of *IOU's*, or social favors, or even political favors, at the fund raiser, Sunday. Then, I'll be on my way, truly, to start anew. Mayor Martin Montgomery is the super sure sound..., which I most want and need to hear right near my ears and others' ears. Now, she's nearing me..., sneering, and, growling.... I really don't want to battle. But, it's going to take far more than just some growl or sneer to stand my damn ground: steady, now, or, just stay steady...!

And, I'm not only shutting my eyes, at present, to avoid the steadily dark, or ugly, and bad scene; which just seems to be utterly unavoidable. But, also, I'm saddling right up, or I'm settling right down, to just fight for what's right. That's so very right! Just, fight with all my goddamn might, tonight—or, whenever...! I throw the light blanket—back, some. Because, it should be right near me—just, in case, I need to cover up, again. Under a little cover, still, I cover right down in order to out-do, and, out-last, and, even, un-cover *Mizani's* real agenda. ...Goddamn that damned woman of a female...! Now, focus, while turning and tossing.... Yet, there's seemingly no time or place to relax or even rest. Stop wig-wagging...!

And, just, fight on...! Or else, I stand to lose all that's so light, pretty, and right, and even good: peace, health, and love, and even happiness, and, of course, success, if not, rest.... Almost, always, obtain, and, retain, and, even, maintain, sure hope, faith, and ambition, and even strength, or staying power: *personal power*. Do so, to get way ahead of, and then stay way ahead of, the starkly, if not, the damnably dark forces or dark powers. They're out there in the near or far distance..., for damn sure. Likewise, they're almost certainly waiting either patiently or impatiently to do me in, expertly. I want and need to be an expert, as well, at fighting, her. Once more, fight on, TROOP! Or, as my Uncle Sam would say..., simply: Carry on, Troop, without your thoughts, rambling, and, roundly. Why doesn't he value some stream of consciousness or some super serious soliloquy...?

Scene 4
The Past

On an unusually cloudy or dim and chilly if not cold yet colorful but—still, a darkly late afternoon in the early spring of 1982; in a nice-sized apartment right near the U.S. Naval Base *Subic Bay*; Petty Officer First Class Martin Montgomery arrives home, wearily, from a day of hard work, so supposedly.

Un-locking and then opening right up the front door of my house, or so-called home, I sense, immediately, that things just aren't right. And, will there be another fight..., tonight? Moving into the apartment, I look around, right quick. I'm looking at various odds and ends that just aren't right. The furniture appears to be very dusty. The carpet even appears to not have been vacuumed. I un-cover, removing my military hat from my head. I don't want some head-ache. But, I've to put my feet forward or down and head-strongly. Just stand my damned ground with the woman, or my seemingly un-loving and un-supportive wife—*Mizani*. I just toss my hat into the wind. But, it just lands on the dirty carpet of a deck. And, I pick it up right quick....

I'm so guessing that our young daughter—or, Maxine is just napping or sleeping. Good! I'm now taking my working jacket off in an effort to get comfortable. Or, to get more comfortable in what's since become an utterly un-comfortable home of a house. I just toss it on the sofa of the living room, my jacket. Looking around, once, again, I notice her book-bag and all. OH, NO! It's another day or late afternoon in which my wife is cutting right into our life, in a very bad way. That she's headed out, un-rightly, to pursue some fabulously fanciful façade of a deliciously good dream: *Mizani* so dreams of becoming an exceptionally educated educator—or, instructor. Please..., just, not, tonight!

I'd like to take off my shoes and then relax, a bit, before dinner. Yet, I think twice or even thrice about it. Since, something tells me, that I may just need to stand super steady in something other than my militarily warm socks. I look up and then down..., stopping, at the love-less love-seat in the living room. That's enough pacing, so un-purposefully. I just flop down on the seat. I see, too, on the clock that's atop the television—that, it's nearing 18:15, or 6:15 p.m. Her class begins at 19:00.... And, I suppose there'll be no stopping *Mizani* from attending it.

I only frown..., and feeling just like a little silly clown. That's since come down from some colorfully cottony clouds.... Their terribly thick mass have clouded, almost, always, the un-colorful, un-candied, and un-seemliness of our marriage. But, no more, which is to say, that was then and this is now. Now, I want or need to be honest, and, harshly. So, honestly, I don't want to fight with her. But, life does have its problems, doesn't it? I wonder is dinner ready to be eaten? For, it takes some super solid food to keep up the damn female-eat-male fight. That's so right, or correct. I just shut my eyes, breathe heavily, and then try to relax. Yet, I'm utterly un-able to do so. Heaviness is wearing or weighing me right down to the ground—or, the utterly un-clean carpet. It needs to be vacuumed, STILL!

Scene 4
The Past
Continued

Right, through my half-open eyes and my semi-consciousness, I see her, *Mizani*. I'm just sitting back on the settee with my head leaning back on its head-rest of sort. She's garbed right in brown-colored gabardine.... It's a short skirt suit of some kind; whose blazer or jacket is pretty padded right at its shoulders. Why've women just taken to having such un-prettily puffy or un-prettily puffed-up shoulders...? Huh...? It's some-what un-becoming, or very masculine-looking, if you're to ask me.... Even *Mizani's* satiny blouse or shirt that's under the jacket is way over-the-top, if you're to ask me.... Its front bow tie is just too damn big. Is it any wonder that such bow tie hasn't smothered *Mizani's* top torso, yet. It's all made-up—her top torso: ...sparkly jewelry—perhaps, a 14-carat-gold necklace, earrings, and all. Of course, I would've given her such super sparklers, and all.

Her legs appear to be bare. But, she wouldn't dare do it! Be all puffed up or dressed up minus stockings. I don't give a goddamn about any weather. For, a real lady ought to always wear a very damn good pair of stockings.... However, *Mizani* is hardly a lady, any more. Her head is almost, always, up in the air and way; whose face is now painted with some gold-looking eye-shadow; and, blackish-brown eye-brows; and, even, brownish-gold lip-stick; that's sparkling just like golden-brown diamonds. I guess that *Mizani* is now some type of diamond in the rough.... Some-times, *Mizani* even believes that she's way tougher than I am.... Plus, I've had just about enough...!

Scene 4
The Past
Continued

Prancing prettily or puffily into the living room, *Mizani* states, "Well, hello there. And, as you know, I'm right on the go. I've class, tonight."

Now, with both eyes open, I just mutter or mumble or even grumble, "Uh-huh." Then, I think to ask, hungrily, "Is dinner ready?"

...Halting at her big and leathern book-bag, *Mizani* replies, roundly, if not rapidly: "Sorry, I just haven't had time to finish it, dinner. I've had lots of home-work..., as you well know.... Also, I've had to ruffle and shuffle with Maxine—or, Maxi, all afternoon. She just came home from her school's field trip..., early." *Mizani* just continues throwing light right upon her supposedly busy goings-on, today. She's doing such, while picking up and straightening out her school-bag...; "Thank goodness that Maxi's sleep..., or, is all warn-out—sleepin'. So, Mister, you can finish dinner and even tidy up things when you're through relaxing—"

Sitting right up, tiredly, I ask, "You're joking, right?"

Mizani asserts, acidly, "No, I'm not jokin' because this isn't the time or the place for any jokes."

Still, she's on the move, moving right—along, in a pair of mid-high heels or pumps…. Her book bag and shoulder bag and all are right in tow. They're all towing right toward the circular mirror that's just hanging on the living room's wall. Once, there, *Mizani* just looks at her-self. She then adds, rather ardently, "I'm off to better my-self with or without your darn help!"

"Woman, please!" I explode, "I'm tired…!"

"PLEASE, don't bark at me…! I'm so darn tired, too, of having this darned back-and-forth run-in with you every other Tuesday or Thursday or even whenever I've class. Or, when you're so tired…. Or, even, when you've some other goddarned pressin' want or need—"

I'm imploding, most, un-prettily, "HOW DARE YOU…!" I shriek—or, explode, again, and seething mad. I even stand up right. I'm just as mad as hell is hot…! I'm about done, as well, tolerating this roundly recognizable woman's so seemingly self-confessed; self-imposed; self-absorbed; and, self-appointed; and, even, self-styled sense; or, the starkly sour siren's super sick sense of responsibility and accountability. Equally, I just aim to hold her very responsible and accountable…, up close, and, in person: "You've since turned right, into a super sensational self-seeker—female; whose super self-seeking thoughts, and words, and ways, more than likely, will be so self-defeating—" I start saying and then pivoting….

Responding, ruthlessly, "SLAP…!" *Mizani* snaps, slapping me right dead on the face with all her damn might.

OUCH! I just want to shout out—loudly. But, I instead slap or smack the fervently fiery female right back…, or just crack, or even snap—my-self: "WHACK…!" I deliver my own damn blow with all my goddamn might!

"You're a miserably selfish bastard!" growls *Mizani,* scowlingly; "If you ever lay another fuckin' filthy finger on me…, you'll live to regret it!"

Glowering, I just retort—or, rebuke, so soundly, and, roundly, "Now you're threatening me, MISSY? HUH? You'll be the one that lives to regret it—"

"Shut the hell up! And, tell me, MISTER, you're happy—now? That you've awaken—Maxi, UH? Answer up—or, better yet, you tend to the darn dinner, and the darn clean up, and even your darn daughter. Since, I'm now finished, fighting, with you…!" *Mizani* orders me, quite gloweringly.

Scene 4
The Past
Continued

Before shuffling, or sashaying, or even strutting off, I just grab hold of her, right quick: or, the rottenly, if not the roundly recognizable woman.... Next, I think better of it. Shoving, or pushing the super self-opinioned siren of a female—hard, on, out the front door, instead. Scowling, I just can't help exclaiming, and soundly, or roundly: "You'll stew stupidly, for damn sure, in your own damned self-aggrandizement, or goddamned self-abasement...!"

Un-touched, or un-moved, outwardly, *Mizani* only moves on—or, she moves right out of my sight.... That's correct—or, right; since, she's now out the front door of my house or my apartment—sight. *Mizani* is moving right along to the outside garage.

There, she'll slide, most definitely, right, into one of my two rides or two cars. *Mizani* will do so, as well, self-consciously, and self-confidently, or self-complacently, yet, still, self-destructively. That god-damn silly or stupid self-seeker of a sure seducer...! She's since learnt absolutely nothing about self-effacement, or humility, and all. Maybe, I'll just let *Mizani* self-destruct, altogether.

Currently, that whining or crying is annoying me, and, absolutely. Per chance, is Maxi doing so because of her parents' voices having been raised, so roundly, and, quite highly? Needless, to say, that I'm mad at *Mizani* and extremely. Yet, the damned female-eat-male fight can't and won't stand in the way of our child's dinner or mine. Thus, I turn to, wearily, yet energetic enough to be a so-called, hungry daddy.

SLAM! I shut the door, at full volume. My most inner strength wants and needs to be waken up, again. Or, be very wide awake and never shake or quake; when, I'm attacked right by the goddamned likes of my un-loving and un-supportive wife of a starkly if not a darkly sharp knife. Focus.

That's right! That once seductively young, shapely, and lovely female of a submissive server; who'd become my damned wife, has since filled my life with such god-damned strife! I'll just have to fight on, and, ferociously, with much height and even more might, for what's light or right in my sight, tonight, or, whenever! Neither can I help wondering has *Mizani*, or that damn seductress seduced some professor of sort—right, with her sensationally slick seductiveness. Focus, now...!

Act IV
Scene 1
The Present
2 Days Later—Saturday

DINNG!

DINNNG, "Goddamit…!" I shriek, being awaken, rudely. And, what damn sound is that…? Is it the alarm clock, or the telephone, or even the door bell? For all three sounds just sound or seem the same, mingling, right, inside my mind; whose utterly unseemly scene still has me as mad as it is hot in hell! *Mizani* has felt, most probably, that I've tried to keep her in some type of damnably dark jail of a very square cell. DINNNG, as it's my little alarm clock that's just sounding, out. I throw the light and bright or white blanket—back, some, reaching for it, alarm clock.

Its super shrill sound sounds right sickening. I'm even feeling a little sick. Since, I'm so damn sick of thinking—or, just, worrying all about my foes' next move, or moves. With a quick tweak of my finger, that shrill sound stops so suddenly. I should stop, too, just, lying here in a saltily stark-naked state of nothingness. Something just has to give way to a brand spanking new day, or Saturday morning. I've planned to tee off or meet up at a nearby golf course with some old comrades of mine. They're so old-school, for sure. This is to say, that the men understand, almost, always, all power structures—or, masculinity, maleness.

I don't like to just toss and turn: or, see-saw back and forth in a super salty and slimy sea of un-certainty. Quite, certainly, I'm turning right over in an effort to get more comfortable. Do so, whilst I continue contemplating my own damn move or moves. Once, I'm at the golf course, I plan to get right down to business. Fund-raise, un-colorfully, yet circularly, and clandestinely. Since, one can never fund raise, enough. It's best to do so, now, while I still have some time before I really start working—or, turning to. I'm now turning back, over, zig-zagging.

Also, I'm seeing over and over, both *Mizani* and Maxi, scheming. Or, they're plotting pretty purposefully their next move or moves: my colorfully circular collapse. Honestly, I want and need to move right to a spanking new address. Put off or push back any further redress by the two: one of whom, I just owe some back alimony to…, still; the second of whom, I just owe some back child-support to…, still; both of whom, still, have been rather un-loving and unsupportive of me; plus, my very big bid to be something far bigger and far better than ever: Damn the two…!

...I'm even trusting that my military buddies' wallets are fatter than ever. They're mostly well employed or well retired; but, still, they're riding so high on their governmental benefits, and all. Perhaps, propping up the two fantastically flat pillows under my head will make me more comfortable. I sit up, un-comfortably, to get more comfortable, for a while longer. It's almost nine o'clock, sharp. Why I'm just feeling something that's super sharp right in my back? Still, I just lie on back in the dark.... I could've turned on a little light. But, what would've been the point?

The big point should've been for me to see, so starkly, the brightness of my prospectively prosperous life minus any damn strife. Fight on, with all my goddamn might, which very well could be with an invisible knife. That's so right. I'm still referring to the seemingly long-lasting and damnably dark sight of my ex-wife and her circularly cold-hearted cohort, or Maxi. The two intend, indeed, to win in the end or ruin my life. I trust, too, that one comrade of mine—in particular, will've a big fat wallet. I want or need to make a big payment toward my so-called family—debt. Do so, before the official launch of my mayoral candidacy on Monday morning.

...What has Sira Simpson since said...? "'...I've never known some damn dead-beat of a politician...'"; That, I just need to hurry up and pay my damned bills.... And, I'll do it without fail...! I doubt seriously if she'll be at the golf course even though such is so feasible. Since, Sira Simpson, sadly, is just another salty, and slimy, or slick, if not a super seductive siren; who, on the surface, likes seducing strong men into thinking that she's submissive and all.

She does so, right, where such men, almost, always, gather, leisurely, or professionally—politically.... Similarly, it's almost certainly about politics or the lack thereof; who's politicking now and later, so purposefully, or not. It just remains a critically central question. Because, some, or most, if not all politicians center their hopes, fears, and the like, more so, on what's to come and less on what's gone by. In other words, they, almost, always, must offer brand new hope, if not constant hope, and so forth, to constituents.

I'm only conveying, and, so circularly, what I do know from personal experience. Having experienced my own pretty and un-pretty politicking, I'm pleased that I've since joined their ranks. I've been a would-be politician—and, a very bona-fide politician—well, I'll become one before long.... That's correct! I can't and won't let anyplace, anything, or anyone just stand in the way of my super sweet success. Once more, it'll be dressed most successfully with very lasting happiness, good health, and genuine love, and even eternal peace. I just need to maintain hope, faith, ambition, and strength, or staying power, or even *personal power*: to just flower pretty powerfully. Wow!

Now, I'm feeling more powerful, so fortunately. I thus sit up and then take stock of my-self: a fantastically fierce fighter; who'll fight on, forever, for what's light, right, and good: GREAT! That, I just can't and won't break my date with fate; or, its gloriously golden gate that opens, rather, goldenly, to a gorgeously gold-colored lake…; where upon I'll just swim in joy, galore. I'm even about to be on the go, to greet Father Fate. But, not before I tidy up, a little, all that's un-tidy: lumpy bed, messy room, and so on.

Scene 2

Clunk! Thump! Clunk! While finishing my tidying up, I just listen to the sound of something or another so thumping, or clunking, away. THUMP! CLUNK! THUMP! Living right on the first floor of this small, and banal, and even two-story building of an utterly unsuitable apartment—or, complex; affords me, many opportunities, more often than not, to just be nosy. GOOD! I'm finished…. Or, things in my bedroom and even elsewhere are tidy, now: or, are all tidy, enough.

So, I make haste, more or less, to just see what's the damn clunking all about. Never mind, too, that's it's stopped—since, or seemingly. I'm still curious…, and am stepping steadily, if not curiously, to my front door. Once, there, I'll take a big peep right out of the door's little peep-hole. It's the same damnably old peep-hole. That so afforded me—at first, a colorfully curious view of Sira Simpson…; then, secondly, an un-colorfully cold, and caustic, if not a very cruel collision of a very vile vision and a very vile visit: Goddamn her…!

Scene 2
Continued

Or, just, goddamn the two…! OH, NO! I'm peeping right through the door's very tiny peep-hole. It's big enough, though, for me to just see Maxine Montgomery. She's stepping right from the right front passenger's side of an old, rusty, and noisy car of some sort—or, an utterly un-colorful clunker…. Needless to say, that I haven't seen my ex-daughter in some time, or months, if not longer. She's wearing a pitch-black-colored and athletic suit of some kind, hoodie, and baggie pants, and even holey sneakers, outwardly.

I wonder what's in the totally tattered tote-bag of hers. Could there be a sharply or a jaggedly dark knife right in it; to just chop right up my mouth-to-mouth life; or just fill it right with darkly stark-naked strife, all over again? I'm not oblivious of Maxi's very new-found height, either. What if she wants to fight me with all her damn might? Or, take a huge and tight or even hellish bite from right out of me? That's right—fight! And, Maxi used to be brighter or lighter. Still, she's some sight, and stepping closer to the front door of my little apartment of a house, home: DAMIT! I want her to disappear…!

Why's *Mizani* just sitting back in the driver's seat of that roundly run-down ride of a car…? And, thankfully, she's since silenced that super sorry-sounding vehicle of hers—or theirs, most, presumably: DAMNIT! I want her to disappear…, also! Yet, it's not happening…. For the two appear, to be not going any damn where. The car is just parked there or right out front. There's no hope, either, of prolonging that which is inevitable. So, should I kiss, or hug her, or even shake one of Maxi's strong-looking hands. She appears to be some type of medium-sized body-builder; who's built up with a strong head, some strong shoulders, a strong body, and all. Maxi even believes, probably, that she has a strong or a big body of evidence concerning my indebtedness or ineptness—uselessness.

Again, it's so inevitable that we just come face to face with each other and then face down one another. It's good, as well, that I've since managed to dis-robe from that holey robe of mine. Now, I'm dressed just fine in a tan-colored and very simple-designed slack set of some kind. Though, the very long-suffering, and moccasin-like, or slip-on shoes—loafers, on my tired feet could sure use some brand new heels. They're wearing right down, because of the utterly unpropitious pressure put upon me by the two. One of whom, is knocking on the front door, presently.

Scene 3

OH, NO…! I just open it right up—or, the front door, so surprisingly. "Oh My…!" I just exclaim—(or, lie), and am not at all surprised to see her, up close—and, in person; "What a surprise it is to see you, Maxine," looking round, about. And, rightly, to see if *Mizani* will be joining her un-surprisingly eye-opening daughter; whose highly high-lighted and sandy-brown-colored hair is just in a pretty plain pony-tail; whose medium-length sits quite well as the sole back-drop of her circularly cute face…; whose deeply peach-colored complexion sits even better—if not, steadier, amidst her super sandy-brown-colored eyes; whose slight slant lies beneath beautifully bushy brows; which are shaped adequately about very high and wide cheeks; whose circularness or circularity still gives way right to a very shinily small mouth; whose sourly steep voice is just about to speak: EEEK or YEEEK…!

…What's this super sub-self-seeker seeking from me…, exactly? Un-rightly, to beat me right down to the ground where upon I'll flounder just like a super silly, white clown…? POUND, for I should've left town, already, or

78

gone downtown, or even elsewhere, anywhere. Somewhere else, that couldn't or wouldn't have me around the damned likes of her, Maxine Montgomery, or my ex-daughter.

"Hi, and I've tried callin', you…," states Maxi, dryly, or sourly, if not resentfully, and stepping forward, steadily, if not rightfully.

"Please, come right in…," I say as a second-thought of sort; "and, I'm sorry, that we haven't spoken, 'or met to settle our damnably dark dispute.'"

Maxi mutters, "Uh-huh," moving forwardly.

Once, Maxi is solidly in my place or my little space…, I just close the door right behind her. Neither should we get too damn close considering all the damnably dark bitterness that's right between us. Nor do I waste any time inquiring…: "Will your mother or *Mizani* be joining us for this little 'or big' visit 'of an utterly unwelcome meeting…?'" and walking right behind my ex-daughter of an intruder. Why's she intruded upon poor and little—me?

Shifting that tattered tote bag or shoulder bag of hers, Maxi answers, "Mother needn't join in our—or, this very necessary meetin'—"

"Oh," I remark, reservedly.

"No. *Mizani* needn't hear what she suspects or knows, by now," Maxi comments. Next, she just moves backward and then forward then sideward, so very disconcertingly. What's her precise purpose for showing up, here, un-announced, and, utterly? "Well, I'll get right to the purpose of my—or, this very over-due visit of mine, or ours…," Maxi starts saying, very wide-eyed; "I'm very well aware of your pretty preposterous, political ambitions. And, if you don't want Mother or me to carry on our colorful, or calamitous, or even catastrophic conversations about you—or, your darkly deep indebtedness to us, in particular. Right, to a roundly respected journalist—then, you'd better pay up. NOW…!"

I'm stunned, some-what, by this roundly recognizable female's stoic, stiff, and steely show of a damned demand. Still, I muster up some stoically stiff steel of my very own to stand my own damn ground on: "So, that's why you're here…?" I question with a super shrill sound and then step up, some. Since, there's really no need to prolong that which is inevitable: Correct?

Stepping up, some, "That's right—or correct!" exclaims Maxi, whose voice rises, soundly, or loudly; "*Mizani* and I both are totally through livin' from hand-to-hand in run-down hand-me-downs! Plus, we're totally through acceptin' all sorts of hand-outs from low-down or hard-up handy-men, who like puttin' their god-damn hands, and all, where they don't even belong!"

After a few seconds or so, Maxi continues, cold-bloodedly, "It takes money to live, Martin. So, DAMIT, hand it over…!"

"I know that—"

"…If you want to go on livin' reasonably well—then, you had better pay up…, NOW! GODDAMIT!" squawks Maxi, with roundly raised brows, and shoulders, and even stance. Why doesn't she just dance away from here, and lovingly, and forgivingly, and even supportingly…? "Neither am I goin' away—or, any where, NOT, until you show me—or us—some real money…, MARTIN! Lots of it is still owed to us—or me, most, specially," adds Maxi, coldly, or acidly. The acid just continues gushing right from her monstrously mealy mouth: "You see—I'm totally through, as I've said—since, of waitin', and waitin', for you, MISTER, to just pay up…! Since, some very serious—back child-support is due right to me. Plus, some very serious—back alimony is due right to *Mizani*—or, right, to your ex-wife." Carrying on, non-sensibly; "who, you've tried, totally, to hold back or take down with some absolutely absurd, or some absolutely asinine idea of submissiveness!"

I rebut, rancorously, and raucously, if not riotously…, "HOW DARE YOU…!"

Shifting that very tattered tote bag of hers, gingerly, "How dare you, MARTIN!" Maxi retorts, acerbically, with acid still surging from her damned mealy mouth; "you god-forsaken and dead-beat of a man—Father!"

With rancor spurting, so soundly, if not roundly, from my own damn mouth, "WHACK…!" I snap and even slap my ex-daughter's face with some super tight might. THAT'S SO RIGHT! I'm not about to just take flight like some goddamned flimsy or weak and white kite. That'll never gain some real height right over some damnably dark fight: "Don't you dare take that tone of voice with me, MISSY! Or, just, continue talking to me rather contemptibly, or quite condemnably…!" I add, acrimoniously, with even more acrimony, or badly black blood boiling all over me. Still, I'll maintain my stance and never once dance to the monstrously misguided music that Maxi is now playing…, most poisonously.

Maxi answers back, and meanly, or maliciously, "Why not…? Since, you're most deserving of a damnably damaged destiny or fate."

"Look here…, CHILD," I now state with nerves that're made of jet-black steel; "I've always intended to just give you and *Mizani*—both, a little something—or, an *I.O.U.*, or a check, or even something else…. For, right now—or, until I can afford to make a really big payment—"

Maxi cuts right in, quite caustically, "Just show me some money—or, *moolah*, MARTIN, RIGHT NOW! Or else—"

"WHAT? What'll you do?"

"Truly, you don't want to know all that I'm truly prepared to do, to ruin you, so roundly!" growls Maxi, scowling, and sourly, or bitterly.

Scene 3
Continued

Now, I only look down and then frown if not glower at this fervently ferocious female of a very damned hound. Time after time, she and *Mizani* both have just hounded me all around—and, right—down: to the dark, dirty, and dangerous, or deleterious, or even deathly ground. So obviously, Maxi is trying very hard to shake up or shake down the sheer steadiness of my flaky foundation; which, my philosophy of life, and the methodology by which I so live it—my own damn life, rests on, and, rather un-easily. I'm now settling down just long enough to offer—but, not, that pleasingly; that, which means the most to my ex-daughter: a monetary payment of some type.

Turning, away, so stoically, I'm just—about, to end this super sick or super sad or even super mad side-show of a show-off or show-down. I alone shall hand-pick the hand-out that I'll hand over, and, some-what, stingily, if not, grudgingly: to the darkly damned descendant of a *Filipino* hand-maid; whose harsh handiwork is most definitely at work, here, today, and, hands-down. Or, I'll just get rid of Maxi before there really be some hand-to-hand combat. Focus, now. Or, produce!

With short yet measured and steady steps, I just continue stepping to a small bookcase that's adjacent to the living room. Its drawers usually contain some of my personal ends and odds. One of which, is my personal checkbook that has a few blank checks in it. Reaching the book case, I just open one of its drawers right up. I'm still so stoic—and, shocked—by my ex-daughter's shocking handity; or, her down-right dexterity in having brought about our big show-down or show-off or even side-show. I'll soon show her or the two that I'm quite serious about reducing my debt…: or, back child-support and back alimony—payments.

By way of luck, I'm very lucky, right now, to have several hundred dollars right in my checking account…. That's because I've yet to pay some other bills, which will come due before long. Damn! I wish that I'd just hold off a while longer…. But, it's not happening…. Since, I'm just about to write out a check for five hundred dollars. I'll do so, too, after I take both my check book and my ink pen from a drawer. But, not, before I steal a quick glance at her, Maxi.

With very fiery eyes and a combative—or, a militant stance, she's just standing by. Neither can I help wondering why Maxi is holding that tattered bag of hers, dexterously. And, of course, she's just looking right down, upon all that means a little something to me: Whether it's a little photograph of my

81

having gotten promoted militarily; or, of my having gotten a little American Flag of a fine souvenir...; or, of my having gotten a little military plaque of recognition, for my outstanding service to my Uncle Sam; all of which, Maxi ought to appreciate without doubt or fail; yet, none of which, appears to mean a damn thing to her. She, who, should know automatically. That, if it weren't for my Uncle Sam..., we all could, and, most likely, would be even more penniless, and powerless.... Still, such hasn't stopped either Maxi or *Mizani* from being some pretty parasitic paupers.... Why haven't the two since learnt something about the very value of a dollar bill and its very basic budgeting? Though, terribly tight that such might've very well been....

Once, I've written out Maxi and *Mizani's* check—(that's so payable to *Mizani*), I put away my ink pen and then my check book, both. Now, her eyes are slanted downward and right on me, rather fierily.

"Just look up and see the pretty positive effort, that I'm now making to negate the situation, 'or this most unpropitious predicament,'" I tell my ex-daughter, accelerating toward her. I want Maxi to leave, right, NOW!

DING-DONG...! Now the doorbell is ringing, so roundly, or soundly. And, without doubt, or fail, it's *Mizani*. She wants to add her left-handed—or, her single-handed handiwork right to this blender of a grinder. Do so even more than before. That's correct! My ex-wife could and would never dream of not grinding me right down..., personally, professionally, and so on. Maxi has since moved on, to the front door of my stiflingly small space. OH, NO! There'll very soon be two suffocating me, seriously, with some more super suffocative demands. Such may even cause me to just do a super or a serious handstand, or even disappear, quite figuratively.

At present, why can't I just be the very late and great Harry Houdini (1874-1926), and perform, perfectly, a disappearing act...? Or, just, put forth, impeccably, a pretty powerful pitch of a plea—deal: Plea most powerfully for some more time.... That'll tell the super sensational story of a pretty princely pauper, and his utterly un-pretty ex-princess of a pretty poisonous pauper—or *Mizani*; who wants badly to pauperize poor me and rather un-prettily, if not quite un-propitiously. Our past life of utterly un-pretty pauperism couldn't be helped, mainly, because of my Uncle Sam's damnably stark stinginess. Also, time has just run out.... It's because Maxi is opening the door, currently. Oh well! It's probably best that I—or, we get outside of my mind or my head, for right now: Focus, DAMNIT...!

The Finale
Scene 4

She looks bad and sad and even mad. Since, *Mizani* is bursting right through the front door of my little house of a home. The now aged, ugly, un-shapely, and un-loving, and even un-supportive; or, the super sour siren of a once submissively seductive seducer or server; wastes no time getting right to the point of this utterly un-inviting visit: "What's taking you so damn long to collect…, Maxi?" questions *Mizani*, leaping right—forward.

Shutting the door right behind her mother or colorfully cozy cohort in crime, Maxi answers. But, not, before she struts toward or alongside *Mizani*; who's since swooped down on me—just, like a very voraciously vile vulture. That's just vying to do away with some prey—me, right away: "Martin is just about to hand over *our* money," states Maxi, moving even closer to *Mizani*.

By the look of their stance, the two are posed purposely, and most un-prettily, for some damn hand-to-hand combat of a dance. Fight. That's right! …They're here to fight me…, on the face of it. "Here…," I tell the two, and handing right over that check for five hundred dollars.

…*Mizani* just snatches it from me and then looks at the check, right, quick. Then, with her eyes bulging; her brows rising; her nose squinting; her mouth pouting; and, her shoulders widening; and, even, her body imploding; *Mizani* explodes, most expressively: "Goddamn you, MARTIN!" and ripping the check, right, up. Its bits and pieces just fall to the ground ever so slow, or slowly. Why can't the two just be on the goddamn go? HEAVE HO!

…I only stare down this utterly un-grateful bitch of an ex-wife; who's standing right before me with her bombastically boorish bastard of a young, or twenty-something daughter. The two are now making me sick, and, super! Blackishly bad blood is boiling over into my eyes right through my head. It's beginning to spin, up, down, around, from side to side, and upside down, and even inside out. The hairs of my eye-brows are curling right up. I can feel it, without doubt. My nose is crunching right down. It's getting hard to breathe. My mouth needs watering. Its dryness is causing some tightness in my throat. I'm just trying to swallow, very hard, some deeply dark dread, and anger, and even worry, or sorrow; all of which has my mind, heart, and body, and even spirit, or soul—imploding. I can't help but to burst out or come apart. I step back, some; yet, still, I stand my damned ground…: "You-all will've to just take it or leave it, another check…!" I inform the two, dryly, yet explosively, enough. Since, I'm now producing…!

Snappily, *Mizani* snaps, "SLAP!" and whacking me right on my right cheek with all her goddamn might.

I'm not about to step back or step down, any more. So, I just step up and then stand my goddamned ground, roundly, and soundly. "GET OUT!" I shriek, loudly, and seething, un-doubtedly. I'm mad since darkly deep dread, worry, and anger, or sorrow—all, are crushing me right down to the ground, or the time-worn tiling: POUND! It's the sound of something un-known—or, so feared, that's just pounding right in my head. It's even starting to go round and round, gyrate, all over again.

Down! I look around and then down at, or, down on the two; both of whom, now have blackish-red-colored fire burning brightly in their wickedly wild-eyed eyes. The fire is ablaze with absolute animosity or horrible hatred. DOWN...! I truly don't want to do it—or, get down—or, take cover. Instead, I only take over.... That's right—or, so very correct! I'm just finished hand-feeding the two hand-made harlots: Damn them...! "GO ON...," I scowl, and frowning, so fantastically; "or, just get the hell out of my house, home! We'll just have to make things right—LATER—"

...Stepping up or over those pieces and bits of a totally torn-up check that's right on the floor of a deck, "You're crazy?" asks *Mizani*. It even looks like she's just about to deck or sack me..., hard, figuratively, if not literally. "WHACK...!" *Mizani* snaps, yet, again, and smacking me right on my left cheek with all her goddamn might.

OUCH! I want to howl right out.

"SLAP...!" *Mizani* is now slapping me even mightier, right, on my right cheek that's still stinging..., on the face of it; "Maxi and I both require at least $1,500—"

I just shove the super seductive siren or soundly sadistic seducer of a once submissive server—on, toward the door, sobbing, sourly: "Just, GO...!" Plus, that's enough of my damned tongue twisting? Because, I've called her out, rightly, or correctly, for the female that she is, *Mizani*.

Scene 4
Continued

Right, through my secondary vision, I just see Maxi sliding sideward. She's laying down, so gently, that tattered tote-bag of hers on the little coffee table.... Why, too, is she so handling it with such damn care...? OH! NO! Is something in there—that, I'd dread, most, definitely? Worry, anger, and the like, are all scaring me, badly, and rightfully. FOCUS, NOW...!

Mizani just shuffles right back and then right toward me, so rumbling, on: "Don't ever push me, AGAIN, MISTER!"

I grumble, or just rumble, "DAMIT…! I said—GO!" and shoving her right forward even more than before.

Now, she's scuffling toward me with roundly raised arms or roundly raised hands and a loudly raised voice…: "Goddamn you, MARTIN!" Maxi protests—or, demands, and then grabbing hold of me with a horribly heavy handgrip; "just, back off—or, away, from my mother, NOW!"

Had I been in my ex-daughter's life, I might've known all about her athleticism: or, her muscled strength. Perhaps, that explains her athletic attire, or garb—get-up, and all. I just shove Maxi off and away from me, hard, and, quite.

"I'LL BE GODDAMNED," *Mizani* squalls, and lunging right at me with some tightly muscled fists of her very own…; "IF I ALLOW YOU TO PUSH OUR—MY DAUGHTER—AROUND! THUMP…!"

"OUCH…!" I screech, and, so seething mad: As, she's just landed a pretty powerful punch upon my person or, poor me. Damn her for having just decked me! More, I'm trying my damnedest to just break free in lieu of being brought down by the two that now have a super strong hold on me. FOCUS! It's a serious hand-spike or some serious leveling that the two have right over me. Also, I see clearly, and very, their very horrible if not their horrific hand-writing that's right on the wall. It's now causing me to fall—or, just, cave in, right, by their damnably dark design.

"DECK…!" Maxi now joins in the punching, and, pretty, powerfully, "SACK…!"

"WHOA…!" I squeal, going down. Maybe, it's because of the utterly unpropitious pressure that I'm now feeling in my chest—or heart, to be exact. The two have only broken my heart into itty-bitty pieces: GODDAMNIT…! …If I were up and about—or, active, I'd most likely whack or even sack the two. And, needless to say, that the two vilely vulturous females are hovering over me…. They're even thinking, quite possibly, that I'm nothing more than damnably disposable debris or utterly un-pretty prey…. It's just so god-damn sickening…!

They're now finished preying right upon me…? It doesn't matter…. Because, I'm totally through fending off the two, or, so it seems to me. That is, I'm now expiring…. My black blood is solidifying. I can feel it, so sadly, and badly. The gyration in my head is now ending…. My brows are curling right down…. My nose is scrunching right up…. My mouth is well watered with super sour saliva. Yet, there's still such tightness in my throat—or, chest of a heart, to be exact.

Nor do I even bother to swallow the darkly deep dread, worry, anger, or sorrow, and all, any more. What would be the point, now? Huh? Since, my mind, heart, and body, and even soul, or spirit are all leaving me far behind. They're taking flight, elsewhere, most seemingly, and leaving the two to only gloat over me…; or, to take pretty perverted pleasure in my timely and total demise…. What's more, will the two now find or have that measure of peace, health, love, and happiness, and even success; that, they've so sought via my own damned well-worn wallet?

Lightness has since turned to darkness. Prettiness has since turned to ugliness. Rightness has since turned to wrongness. Goodness has since turned to badness, and so on. On my eye-lids, too, are two, crooked, and diamond-shaped tears that've yet to fall from grace, gracefully. I can feel their sizable fear, some-what, of the two ferocious females…. They're still hovering right over me, so ungracefully, and utterly. Good-bye and goddamn good riddance to my sad ex-wife, and, to my mad ex-daughter: the bad!

Scene 4
Continued

Mizani just bellows with big bulgy eyes: "Maxi!"

Speechless, Maxi is just hovering over me with slantingly bulgy eyes of her own—frozen, fundamentally.

"MAXI…!" *Mizani* hollers, again, un-freezing her daughter; "Don't just stand there—so mute—do somethin'…! Check his pulse—OH GOD…! What's happened? Why's Martin just lying there—so life-less? See—"

"O.K.!" squeals Maxi, stooping, slowly, and very.

I, Martin Montgomery, a would-be, ex-military, and, a so-called—up-standing man of a would-be politician; or, a starkly dark dead-beat, am just lying here…: outwardly—expressionlessly; plus, outwardly—listlessly; and, even, outwardly—voicelessly…; having since been over-taken by an overtly over-powering, and a nakedly grayish-dark sea of stark-naked nothingness…. What's truly causing me to just lie here in such a super sick state…? Huh…? Per, chance, is it darkly bad health or even something else…? Had I taken a physical—maybe, then, I would've known my very true status, medically. I shouldn't have put it off for so very long. Truthfully, I've been meaning to do such, soon, and, very. If only I were up and about or mobile…!

Now, Maxi just wants to know such answer, so apparently, about my life-less-ness…: lack of health—or, get-up-and-go. She stoops down low and then bends over, some. Then, she checks my pulse on both sides of my neck; however, to what damn avail…, uh? Next, she looks up, so slowly, at *Mizani*,

86

and then shakes her head from side to side. All the while, Maxi is doing so, speechlessly.

"Well?" *Mizani* just pumps Maxi for unanswerable answers, possibly; "Well? Is he alive—or, breathin'? What's wrong...?"

"His pulse is awfully weak. I'll check his breathin'—"

"YES! Do that while I call 911...! OH, GOD! What's happened...?" questions *Mizani*, and even dashing away...; "...Check again—his pulse—or wrists...!"

...Having knelt down, a little more than before, Maxi is now listening right for my breath or my breathing—faint, though it may very well be. Her now performing cardiopulmonary resuscitation (or CPR) is next in order, so observably, yet, *quite, questionably*. Tilting my forehead and my jaw both—back, some; and, then, blowing, two, so-called rescue-breaths into my mouth, some; then, doing, some, so-called chest-compressions—all, to what damn or actual avail? Huh?

That's right! I'm not smelling, or hearing, or even feeling, nor tasting, but seeing such—all, right, through my half-open eyes; or, right, through my super semi-consciousness...; or, even, right, through my starkly sick state of being. I also know..., because her touch and all is hardly real, Maxi's. Sadly, or sickly, I can even taste the super wetness, or the super dryness, or even the super sourness, of this super sad, or super sick situation, still. Yet, I ought to just let go. Or, I ought to just give my own damned self the HEAVE-HO! So, what would be the point of living in a dark, if not a hot and an un-forgiving—or, an in-escapable, yet, rather welcoming—hell, uh? Since, I'm dying inside to some goddamned avail! HO! HO! HO!

Scene 4
Continued

...Having since dashed to the telephone, that's atop a little end table; that's next to the couch; her voice is now sounding out, so stridently: "Hello! HELLO! Help! Please! I need an ambulance—QUICK!" *Mizani* cries out; "I don't know...! HELP! PLEASE! And, HURRY! OH! DEAR GOD—what's wrong—" the beggar just begs on, for that which may very well be too damn little and too damn late. Since, I'm barely holding on, to life. It's a life, that may very well be un-worthy of living, and, so utterly. Could life just be lived much better in the after-life, or the here-after, or even the next world? I sure hope so, as I'm now journeying there without doubt or fail.

"...SLAM...!" *Mizani* slings the telephone right down on its receiver. Then, she dashes right back, to the scene of their crime, hers, and Maxi's....

"The ambulance is on the way…! I pray to God, too, that Martin will live—" *Mizani* starts to say yet is cut right off.

Maxi responds, "I doubt it…," and, just, rising up, at a damnably old snail's pace; "I've done CPR—or, cardiopulmonary resuscitation. It's all that can be done—"

"If he dies—well, we've acted in super sure self-defense!"

"Thank goodness—or God, too—that our big fight and all is right on tape," offers Maxi.

"Yes," agrees *Mizani*. She then moves very hastily toward that totally tattered tote-bag of Maxi's.

Now, Maxi is moving just as hastily toward their so-called evidence. Evidently, there's a tape recorder of some sort in such bag. "Sure enough…," *Mizani* comments, and taking the little recorder right from Maxi's tote bag…; "Thank you, LORDY…!" she exclaims, seeing, and hearing its super snaky sound.

"…Re-wind it, right, QUICK!" Maxi requests—or demands—or even orders; "So that it'll be ready right when the cops—or, the ambulance, and all—get here!"

"INDEED!" *Mizani* proclaims, "We'll have some super solid proof of our innocence—just, in case, it's wanted or even needed. There's no doubt— that, Martin intended to whack and sack us—both! Truthfully, he gave me a super scary shove of a darkly damned scare, and all—"

"YEAH…!" Maxi concurs…, and, most circularly, "I was just getting super scared my own damn self! Still, we'll just have to let the tape tell the sourly, if not the solidly sordid story of Martin's down-right down-come, or collapse. However, I tend to think that it's a serious—medical issue—"

"Like what?" queries *Mizani*, and securing the tape recorder…, quite, gingerly.

"I'm not rightly sure—but, it could be an organ failure…. OH, GOD! What if one of our whacks or decks was the cause of his cavin' in—"

In a terribly tense tone of voice, *Mizani* retorts, roundly, or soundly: "NO…! It just can't be…!" and then placing the tape recorder right down on the little off-centered coffee-table; "And, just, between you and me—or, us," she continues, and seemingly, rather nervously…; "most, possibly, Martin is well deserving of his very present fate that's been draped, almost, always, in utterly untenable tragedy, heart-break, or heart-ache."

"Yeah, I suppose so…," Maxi comments…, quite, nonchalantly, yet, interestingly, "and I'm reminded, roundly, of an old sayin'—"

"What?" *Mizani* asks, and trying to comfort Maxi, most presumably, by hugging her.

"Well....," states Maxi, super stoically, "just, because somebody could or *can* help you—such, doesn't mean, so necessarily, that *she* or he would or *will* help you...."

Wordlessly, *Mizani* only looks at Maxi, askew, or cock-eyed. They'll have to talk, and obviously, or inevitably, about this very deathly or death-like incident of a not so far-fetched or fanciful or even fantastic fight. That's so correct—or, right! It's just so very dark...!

Prior to my fantastically frail or faint heart-beat dying out; I, Martin Montgomery, still, sense the super sour sourness of the two females' undying repulsion—or, their horrible hatred of me. Boo, hoo! Neither am I sad, at all, to be just about through with the two...: or, "the Bad." After all, it's not my damn fault if *Mizani* has failed, and, rather miserably; to bring her fabulously fanciful façade of a decidedly or even a deliciously good dream to reality or actuality.

But, instead, she's since suffered nothing more or less than a pretty perverted or a super Shakespearean tragedy. Like, most, if not all of William Shakespeare's (1564-1616) very central characters. That've, inherently, some characteristically tragic flaw; which, almost, always, is the circular cause for her or his fall or even down-right down-come, perversity. That's so right, or correct...! *Mizani* could've only dreamt of being an exceptionally educated educator or instructor; who, quite feasibly, or quite un-prettily, would've only used her students, so perversely, as super solid step-ladders: right, to a more secure future, or, a much better life. Like, so sadly, how she's since used her own damned daughter..., pretty pervertedly: god-damned un-pretty pervert!

Once, more, I just want to shout right out...: Good-by and god-damn good riddance...! Instead, the super shrill sounds of nearby sirens sound out, deafeningly. What's more, it's no big secret that the good—and, the bad love each other despite their hatred of one another. The good being an ambulance that in-arguably wants to save my life...; and, the bad being these, two utterly unfeminine females that could care less, so arguably, if I were dead and most definitely. This is to say, at this instant, that it's quite enough of prolonging an inevitably extended end...; or, an utterly un-pretty perversion...; or, even, my super soliloquy, so soliloquizing, and solidly...: Now, UN-FOCUS...! Or, just let the damn aching—or, heart-ache, just, ache, right, away. Do so, right, as my non-productive production or productivity just ceases to wig-wag, or zig-zag, or even see-saw.

The End

Why juxtapose two of life's biggest dichotomies: or, the good and the bad? For the two—the bad, and the good—almost, always, feed upon each other; while at the same time spew out one another; while at the same time—still, get right back, together. In essence, it is a very seemingly surrealistic or sadistic but sufferable yet nonetheless, a somewhat sick—or, an up and down and all-around cycle; in lieu of such, has some merit albeit such is warped, most likely. In order for us to analyze, and realize, and even rate what lies at the core of the two, or the good and the bad; it is first necessary for us to look internally instead of externally or even else where. To trace what may very well motivate the two: Their ulterior motives or even the lack thereof, which, almost, always, will be all about virtues and vices or the lack there of—will it not?

So, consequently, ethics and its ability to just effectuate certain moral principles; plus, morality and its ability to just alter conduct; whose behavior could be either right or wrong and motives either good or bad; all of which, ultimately, determines character, or one's being: the collectively colorful or colorless characteristics of one's person or even personality. It is necessary, likewise, for us to appreciate both the philosophy and the methodology of the two; or, the good and the bad—and, so, in particular, what is at their interior; which cause them to obtain, and retain, and even maintain life's very basics or the lack thereof: hope, faith, and, ambition, and, even, strength, or, staying power—*personal power*: commitment, perseverance, and, courage, and even honor: peace, health, love, and, happiness, and, even, success. I have so tried, even, right, through the use of certain artistic, creative, and literary tools, to effectuate both the bad and the good—or, two short stories; where by, we are not just abstracted and beguiled but even enlightened right by the two: very long short stories—or, novellas—or, even, "The Good," and "The Bad," as it were, so respectively. And, to be so—right, through first person narratives, or even point of views (*P.O.V.'s*); which are rather restricted to what exactly the central/peripheral narrators can see and sense, quite sensibly.

Subsequently, the natural need for some bona-fide balance is usually necessary when juxtaposing some dichotomy, so artistically; hence, the good and the bad, or the very two titles and even their circularly clear contrast—or, down-right dis-similarity. Such juxtaposition is very well served, particularly, when drawing references, inferences, interpretations, conclusions, and the like; all of which are relevant, and, roundly. The scenery or setting is equally important. For, it is where we ought to see some kind of spot-light, or high-light—special hue; coloring the story in a specific way or some other way or even another way, specifically. That is, amid the story's setting, or colorful, or even colorless back-drop—or, back-ground, there must be a focal-point; at which point, your eyes are drawn, voluntarily; or, drawn so in-voluntarily, or even purposefully, by the narrator, or me—the anonymous author, ultimately.

More, in the midst of such purpose, or the drawing of your attention in one way or another way or even some other way; most, certainly, you do not want to miss certain artistic emblems; whose accents, more than likely, will suggest if not solidify the short stories' themes or motifs. Besides such, there is almost, always, some symbolism or imagery infused with those same artistic accents, or, emblems; which adds some substantial substance to the subject matter or, motif—theme: Whether they are real or made-up symbols or even images; that are so contrastively colorful, dark, or some where in between, or even else where. Through out the short story, or, two, long short stories, as it were, we will find the colorful or the colorless use of language; whether it is figurative, literal, or otherwise, as well as descriptions that are either very real or very imaginative; all of which just adds to such creativity or creativeness: the originally creative process.

Further, there is a very natural need for some real balance, creatively, when juxtaposing some of life's biggest dichotomies: like, hope and despair; faith and doubt; ambition and sloth; strength and weakness; commitment and mis-obligation; perseverance and submission; courage and cowardice; honor and disgrace; peace and pother; health and sickness; love and heart-break; pleasure and pain; happiness and sadness; success and failure—or, gains and losses, and so forth. Such juxtaposition is well served—still, when creating certain references, inferences, and, interpretations, and even, conclusions; all of which, expectantly, helps to foster critical or higher-order-thinking skills. Whether the mechanisms are so creatively colorful, or colorless emblems, or accents, or even symbols, and so on; all of which, when mixed contrastively with the allegorical and metaphorical use of language or semantics; can and does take on several creative forms that are inherently rhythmical, repetitive, rhetorical, or otherwise.

Furthermore, such sonance or the use of very deliberate sound in either written or spoken language, almost, certainly, brings about, and then reinforces even more engagement: or, a Reader's participation right in the reading process. To enrich the reading experience, I, almost, always, insert independently subjective questioning; or independently objective questioning of the subject-matter, or even some sub-matter; which, more often than not, so impels a Reader to engage, educationally, his or her critical and creative-thinking processes, or skills: for example, problem-solving; decision-making; designing; analyzing; evaluating; connecting; synthesizing; elaborating; imagining; theorizing; and, strategizing, and even more; all of which, allows a Reader—or you, to some-what season some real—artistic, and creative, and even literary—personal self-discovery, or self-realization: a truly meaningful measure of characterization; whose moral principles and conduct both reflect, so roundly, a certain intellectuality, morality, and spirituality—in time, if not, right away.

What is more…, such intellectually cognitive, morally affective, plus spiritually physical—or psycho-motor, or engagement, if not enlightenment, or clarification; will—most likely, at the end of the day, just, precipitate, and then perpetuate a very certain philosophy of life and methodology by which it ought to be so lived: self-discovery, or, self-realization; whose ethics, and, morality, and even character, or principles, and methodologies—all; will lead right to a great measure of having, and retaining, and even maintaining hope, faith, and, ambition, and, even, strength, or, staying power, (*personal power*): commitment, perseverance, and courage, and even honor: peace, health, love, happiness, and success, and even more—gains—collectively. To truly coddle and even conquer the very multi-educational endeavor of climbing, right, up the taxonomy of higher-order-thinking skills, or processes: problem-solving, decision-making, designing, and the like.

Therefore, almost, always, decide whatever some problem is or is not. Then, just design a solution right to the problem if it exists. Then, just make a decision concerning the probable solution or plan. Then, just analyze the plan or resolution. Then, just evaluate the resolution or decision. Then, connect the decision or assessment right to the problem or even something else that is applicable. Then, synthesize or blend the evaluation anew. Then, stipulate or elaborate on the new valuation. Then, imagine or visualize the new appraisal. Then, theorize or hypothesize the new review. Then, strategize or organize the new resolution's execution; all of which has brought me, finally, to my own strategy, having strategized right through my writings. In other words, I have written artistically, creatively, and, literarily—or, right, on purpose: to affect your cognitive, affective, and psychomotor—domains.

Thus, the three to four, or main domains, or even main categories of mental, emotional, and physical, and even spiritual being; as it were, are what I have so tried to lay emphasis on, here, and else where: To have done so in various ways, mainly, via a bi-layered, if not a multi-layered and personable theme; which, largely, Readers can relate to, so universally, or identify with, with-standing certain idiosyncrasies that are so in-bred, individually. Still, the very universal up and down and forward and backward and even sideward movements of life's challenges: or, even, digressors, regressors, repressors, and oppressors, and even successors, and so forth; all of which, sometimes, if not, oftentimes, just, create colorful or colorless conflicts—not, just, between or among others—but, even, right, with-in one-self. One only needs to get right through the bad to get right to what is good or great. Do so, steadily, if not, at first, smartly, and strongly, and even successfully. Yet, do such, at any rate, without doubt, or fail.

Lastly, commitment, and perseverance, and even courage are almost, always, required; that, and having steady hope, faith, and ambition, and even strength—or, staying power: *personal power*. Such might and all is almost certainly compulsory, to just conquer life in one way or another way or even some other way. That is right! To conquer life just like a certain conqueree, having turned conqueror conquering that that has been un-conquerable. It is, equally, a pleasurable process, plus a painful process; or, a certainly circular conquest that just has to be conquered, and, quite circularly, without doubt—or, fail.

Last of all, have I my-self failed in my circular quest to be some-what of a consummate writer; who has since written, un-colorfully, colorfully, and circularly, and even capably, enough? In any case, as I am ending this—or, my many years of writing(s); which has been a staggeringly huge, and, an evolutionarily educational endeavor—(for me, especially); once more, I most certainly thank each and every Reader of my book(s); for permitting me the privilege of diverting your attention; and, beguiling you; and, even, allowing me to put right into words, my "own" artistic, creative, and literary logic—or, voice: whether rhythmical, repetitive, rhetorical, or otherwise; all of which, just, has a roundly recurrent theme or very similar subject and will continue to have such, without doubt, or fail.

www.ingramcontent.com/pod-product-compliance
Lightning Source LLC
Chambersburg PA
CBHW081148170626
46809CB00010B/3130